Eleanor Roosevelt

Fighter for Social Justice

Illustrated by Gray Morrow

Eleanor

Roosevelt

Fighter for Social Justice
By Ann Weil

Aladdin Paperbacks

Aladdin Paperbacks
An imprint of Simon & Schuster
Children's Publishing Division
1230 Avenue of the Americas
New York, NY 10020
First Aladdin Paperbacks edition, 1989
Printed in the United States of America

10 9 8 7 6 5 4 3

Library of Congress Cataloging-in-Publication Data
Weil, Ann, 1908–
    Eleanor Roosevelt: fighter for social justice/by Ann Weil. — 1st Aladdin
Books ed.
    p. cm. — (The childhood of famous Americans series)
    Reprint. Originally published: Eleanor Roosevelt: courageous girl.
Indianapolis: Bobbs-Merrill, 1965.
    Summary: The childhood of the woman who became a great humanitarian
and wife of a president.
    ISBN 0-689-71348-7
    1. Roosevelt, Eleanor, 1884–1962—Juvenile literature.   2. Roosevelt,
Eleanor, 1884–1962—Childhood and youth—Juvenile literature.   3.
Presidents—United States—Wives—Biography—Juvenile literature.
[1. Roosevelt, Eleanor, 1884–1962—Childhood and youth.   2. First ladies.]
I. Title.   II. Series.
E807.1.R48W42   1989   973.917'092—dc20
[B]   [92]   89-37781   CIP   AC

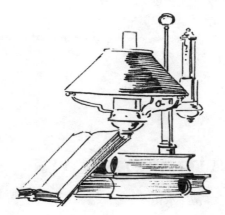

To
Steven and Alan

Illustrations

Full pages

Numerous smaller illustrations

Contents

★ ★ ★

★ # Eleanor

Roosevelt

Fighter for Social Justice

Eleanor Visits
Hyde Park

LITTLE ELEANOR Roosevelt sat on a bench in the hallway and swung her feet back and forth. Now and then she stopped, held her legs out straight in front of her, and looked at her shoes. She had on her best hat, coat, and shoes.

"Going visiting," she sang. "Going visiting."

"Hello, Little Nell."

Eleanor looked up and saw her father and mother coming down the stairs. Her mother walked slowly, holding up one side of her long skirt so it would not drag on the carpet. Her father ran down the stairs two steps at a time and caught her up in his arms.

"We're ready," he said. "Now let's see whether James and the horses are ready."

He opened the big front door and there, on the driveway, stood a coachman, a carriage, and two horses.

"Good morning, Mr. Roosevelt." The coachman touched his whip to his cap.

"Good morning, James."

Still holding Eleanor in his arms, Mr. Roosevelt walked around to the front of the horses. "Good morning, Lady. Good morning, Jack."

The horses snorted and tossed their heads and stamped the ground with their hoofs.

"There. There." Mr. Roosevelt patted each horse. "Steady, now. Steady." He took a piece of sugar out of his pocket and held it up close to Lady's mouth. In a second a big, red tongue had licked it up.

"Now, you do it." Mr. Roosevelt gave Eleanor a piece of sugar.

Eleanor was afraid when the horses snorted and tossed their heads. She didn't want that big red tongue licking at her fingers.

"Come on. Don't be afraid. I gave mine to Lady. You give yours to Jack."

Eleanor began to open her hand very slowly. Frightened, she started to close her fingers again. Then the big tongue reached out and the sugar disappeared. Eleanor laughed. The tongue had tickled her fingers.

Mr. Roosevelt climbed into the carriage and put Eleanor gently on the seat between him and her mother. "Off we go," he said, nodding to the coachman.

Eleanor liked sitting in the big coach between her mother and father. The ride lasted for a long time, but finally the coach stopped in front of a large house.

"We are going to visit a lady whose last name is the same as ours—Roosevelt," explained Mrs.

Roosevelt. "She has a little boy, named Franklin. He's a distant cousin of yours, and your father is his godfather. The town, near where they live, is called Hyde Park."

"That's right," Mr. Roosevelt said. "It's a good idea to start telling her about all the Roosevelt families. Perhaps when she's our age she'll have them straightened out."

Mrs. Roosevelt laughed. "I know she doesn't understand a word I'm saying," she answered, "but she looks so solemn and wise I forget she's only two. Anyway," she added, "I think people should talk to children as if they actually understand what you're saying to them."

Mr. Roosevelt nodded. "Especially to this one," he said. "Come on, my wise little owl. Perhaps you understand more than we think."

Inside the big house, Eleanor's mother and father walked into a large drawing room. They shook hands with a lady and a little boy, but

Eleanor stopped at the doorway. Mrs. Roosevelt held out her hand to her little daughter.

"Come in, Granny." Then, smiling, she turned to her hostess and said, "Eleanor is such a shy little girl. She's always so solemn and—and—well, rather old-fashioned looking. That's why I call her Granny."

"And I call her Little Nell," Mr. Roosevelt added, "after the Little Nell in one of my favorite books, Dickens' *Old Curiosity Shop*."

While they were talking, Franklin walked over to Eleanor and looked down at her. "I'm five years old," he said. "How old are you?"

"Oh, she's only two," Mr. Roosevelt answered. "She isn't old enough to understand a question like that."

"Can't she say anything?" Franklin bent down until his face was level with Eleanor's. "Can't she talk at all?"

"Oh, yes." Mr. Roosevelt walked over and

stood beside the two children. "She can say quite a few words. I made a list of them the other day, and there were almost three hundred. But, you see, she doesn't understand about things like birthdays and people's ages."

Franklin stood up. He felt very grown-up beside this little girl. "Is she just going to stand there all day?" he asked. "Isn't she ever going to say anything or do anything? Won't she play with me?"

"She's very shy, especially with people she's never seen before," Mr. Roosevelt explained. "After a little while perhaps she will——"

Franklin didn't wait for Mr. Roosevelt to finish. He dropped down on his hands and knees. Then, looking at Eleanor, he said, "See, I'm a horse." He tossed his head and kicked his heels in the air. "Do you want to go for a ride?"

Eleanor looked at Franklin. Then, opening her hand, she held it close to his face.

16

Mr. Roosevelt laughed. "She fed one of the horses some sugar just before we left home," he said. "I suppose she thinks you might like some sugar, too. You see, she isn't old enough to understand many things, but she does know how to pretend sometimes. Perhaps she wants to show you that she thinks you are a nice, friendly horse and she isn't afraid of you." Then, bending down, he lifted Eleanor and put her on Franklin's back.

"Now put your arms around his neck," he said, "and hold on tight."

At first Franklin walked very slowly, but after a little while he began to go faster and faster. Soon both of them were rolling on the floor.

"Franklin!" His mother hurried across the room. "You must be careful. She is just a little girl. You might hurt her."

Franklin jumped up. "Did I hurt you?"

Eleanor shook her head. Then, clapping her

hands, she began to jump up and down. "More! More!" she cried. "More! More!"

Franklin got down on his hands and knees again, and this time Eleanor wasn't afraid to climb on her "horse" all by herself.

After a while a maid came in with a large tray containing sandwiches and cakes. There was tea for the grownups and milk for Eleanor and Franklin. Then it was time to go home.

"Well, Little Nell," said Mr. Roosevelt, when they were in the carriage again, "do you enjoy going visiting?"

Eleanor wasn't sure what visiting meant, but whenever   was with her father, everything seemed to be all right. She wasn't afraid of horses, or strange houses, or people she didn't know. She wasn't even afraid of a little boy who pretended he was a horse. Looking up at her father, she nodded her head. Then, leaning against his shoulder, she went sound asleep.

Going to Europe

ELEANOR SAT on a bench in the hallway, waiting for her parents. The hallway was filled with big, round-topped trunks, leather hat boxes, and wicker baskets.

Once again Eleanor had on her best clothes. This time, however, she was five years old, and now she had a little brother named Elliott Roosevelt, Junior. Mr. and Mrs. Roosevelt, Eleanor, her little brother, and their nurse, Nancy, were all going to Europe.

Her father tried to explain to Eleanor what going to Europe meant. "Europe is made up of many different countries," he said, "just as the

20

United States is made up of many different states. We are going to three European countries—England, France, and Italy."

Then Mr. Roosevelt showed Eleanor a big map. "See," he said, " all the part that is colored blue is the ocean. We're going to go across that ocean in a big ship. This country, which is colored green, is England. The pink one is France, and the yellow one is Italy."

Eleanor nodded. She hoped she understood about oceans, countries, colors, and maps, but she wasn't sure. She was only sure of one thing. It all sounded exciting and wonderful.

In a few minutes Nancy came with little Elliott, and James followed with packages.

"Well! Well!" Mr. Roosevelt looked around at all the luggage that almost filled the hallway. "I just hope the ship doesn't sink when we put all these things on it."

Eleanor looked up, frightened by what her

father had said. Suddenly she remembered something she hadn't thought about in a long time, and she began to tremble.

Once, when she was only three, she and her parents had started to Europe on another big steamer. It was foggy, and before they were out of the harbor a large boat ran into their ship. First there was a loud crash, followed by a great deal of noise and confusion. People screamed and shouted and ran about the decks, not knowing where to go.

A sailor picked up Eleanor and held her over the side of the ship. Far below she could see her mother sitting in a little boat and her father standing with his arms outstretched. "Don't be afraid," he had shouted to her. "I'm going to catch you. Don't be afraid."

But Eleanor was afraid. She had never been so frightened in her life. The boat looked small and far away. It bobbed up and down in the tall waves, and at times it seemed to disappear altogether. Eleanor wasn't sure her father would be able to catch her. What if he couldn't catch her and she fell into that big, black ocean filled with high waves?

Eleanor had screamed and kicked and held onto the sailor as tightly as she could. She didn't care what happened to her as long as he didn't drop her over the side of the ship. Suddenly she felt herself falling through the air— down—down—down—and then, at last, she wasn't falling. She was in her father's arms.

"There, Little Nell. You're all right now." Mr. Roosevelt tried to comfort her. "See, I caught you, just as I said I would. You're safe now. Nothing is going to happen to you."

Eleanor knew she was safe. She knew her father was holding her and everything was all right. But she couldn't stop crying. As the little boat took them back to shore she could think of only one thing. Terrible things happened on ships, and she would never go on one again. Never! Never! Never!

A month later Mr. and Mrs. Roosevelt made plans to go to Europe on another ship, but Eleanor refused to go. Whenever they talked about it she kicked and screamed, remembering the night the sailor had dropped her over the side of the ship.

"I won't go on a ship," she cried, stamping her foot. "I won't! I won't! I won't."

Finally her parents decided to let her spend the summer with her aunt instead. Two years had passed since that frightful night, but she still remembered all the terrible things that had happened after the accident.

"Oh, Papa! Do you think the ship might sink? Do you really think it might?"

Mr. Roosevelt stooped down and put his arm around her shoulders. "I'm sorry," he said.

"That was a foolish thing to say. I was only teasing. This luggage won't make a bit of difference on the big ship.

"You must not be afraid of ships. Thousands and thousands of ships have crossed the ocean safely. Don't be afraid. People who are afraid never do anything interesting and exciting. Don't you remember what I told you about the ship we're going on?"

Eleanor nodded. Her father had told her the ship would be like a big hotel that would carry them across the ocean. Thinking about it made her feel excited again. Anyway, if her mother and father and little brother were going, she wanted to go with them.

Taking her father's hand she began to pull him toward the door. "Come on, Papa," she said. "We don't want the ship to go off without us. Let's hurry as fast as we can."

The Big Ship

FOUR CARRIAGES were needed to take the Roosevelts, the servants, and the luggage to the ship, but at last all were ready to go. Usually Eleanor liked nothing better than to ride in a carriage, but today she was eager for the ride to end. She was too eager to see the big ship to think of anything else.

Finally the carriage stopped in front of the docks and everyone got out. Mr. Roosevelt lifted Eleanor from the carriage and put her down on the wooden dock. "I want you to walk up the gangplank by yourself," he said, "because walking up the gangplank of a big ship is wonderfully exciting. As you walk, you say good-by to buildings and streets, to yards and parks, and to horses and carriages. For eight days you are going to live in a world which has none of these things. A ship is a tiny world which moves across the blue ocean the way the sun seems to move across the blue sky."

The gangplank was steep, and the slats, which were nailed across it to keep people from slipping, were far apart. At least Eleanor had trouble reaching them with her short little legs. Sometimes her feet slipped as she stepped from slat to slat. However, her father never offered her his hand, and she knew he would be disappointed if she asked him for help.

When they reached the top of the gangplank Mr. Roosevelt once more lifted Eleanor up into his arms and walked over to the railing. Then, suddenly, the air was filled with long, brightly-colored streamers. The people on the ship were throwing the streamers toward the people on the dock. Some of them sailed through the air, some floated on the water, and some fell down the side of the ship.

Eleanor looked at her mother. Some of the streamers had fallen onto her hat and over her hair. Mrs. Roosevelt laughed as she brushed them aside, but Eleanor thought they made her look more beautiful than ever. She looked like a fairy princess—a beautiful fairy princess with green and pink and purple hair.

After this a strange thing happened. The dock and all the people on it seemed to move away from the ship. They moved farther and farther away until they looked only half as large as they had before. Eleanor turned around and looked over her father's shoulder. Then she saw that the dock wasn't moving away from the ship. The ship was moving away from the dock. The Roosevelts were on their way to Europe.

The ship was like a hotel. There were bed-rooms, but Eleanor learned that on a ship they were called cabins or staterooms. There were porches, but they were called decks. There were kitchens, but they were called galleys. There was a basement, but it was the hold, and the stairs were called companionways. There were windows, but they were called portholes.

Eleanor learned that the front of the ship was called the bow and the back was called the stern. She learned, too, that the left side of the ship was called the portside and the right side was called the starboard. When her parents took her to see the captain of the ship he was in a kind of balcony which extended over the top deck. But it wasn't called a balcony. It was called the bridge.

One day when Eleanor and her mother were sitting in their deck chairs, Mrs. Roosevelt started to talk to a passenger who was sitting next to them. Eleanor listened carefully, but after the woman left she said to her mother, "I listened and listened, but I couldn't understand a word that you and that other lady said."

"The other lady is French," Mrs. Roosevelt explained, "and people who live in France speak a different language. That means that they use different words than we do. In France the people speak French."

"What language do I speak?"

"You speak English."

"And you can speak English and French?"

"Yes, I learned to speak French when I was a little girl."

"Can Papa speak English and French, too?"

"Yes, he can."

Eleanor thought for a few minutes. Then she said, "I can speak two languages, too."

Mrs. Roosevelt looked surprised. "You can? What two languages can you speak?"

Eleanor looked around her before she answered. Then she said, "Oh, you know, Mama. Now that we are on a ship we use different words for everything, just the way you say they do in France. Words like porthole and galley and starboard and stern—words like that."

Mrs. Roosevelt laughed, and even after she started to talk her mouth seemed to want to smile. "You're right," she said. "There are a great many special words to describe things on a ship. They are called nautical words."

"Nau-ti-cal?" Eleanor pronounced it slowly. This was another new word. "Then—then do I speak nautical?"

Mrs. Roosevelt smiled again. "You speak nautical very well. But tomorrow you will have to start speaking nothing except English again."

"Why?"

"Because tomorrow we are going to land in England."

"Then we won't be on the ship anymore?"

"No. Tomorrow we leave the ship and go to a large city called London."

"London." Eleanor repeated the word as if it were a new flavor that she was tasting for the first time. "London." She wondered if she would like London.

"Is London like New York?" she asked.

"No," Mrs. Roosevelt answered. "It's different. It's very different. Wait and see."

At that moment the captain of the ship passed by and stopped to speak to them. Then, as he turned to leave, Eleanor climbed out of her deck chair and tugged at his coat sleeve.

"I know something very important," she said. "Would you like for me to tell you what it is?"

The captain stopped and looked down at her.

"Yes," he said. "I would very much like for you to tell me something important."

Eleanor stood up very straight. The telling of

important news was a serious matter. "Tomor-row," she said, looking very solemn, "tomorrow we are going to land in England. I thought you would like to know."

"Thank you very much for telling me. I——"

but before the captain could say anything more, his face began to get very red. He looked as if he was going to choke. Taking his handkerchief out of his pocket, he began to cough.

"I'm really very pleased that you told me," he said when he could speak. "Very pleased."

Then, smiling at Mrs. Roosevelt, he said, "I must go to the bridge at once. If the news that this young lady just told me is really true," he smiled again, "well, I have a great many things that I must do before tomorrow."

"Everyone smiles at you, Mama, because you are so pretty," Eleanor said, after he left.

"Thank you, Eleanor. That is a very nice compliment, but I don't think the captain was smiling because he thought I was pretty."

Eleanor thought for a moment. Then she said, "Do you think he was just being polite?"

"Yes, that's right." Mrs. Roosevelt nodded. "He was being polite, very polite."

Travel Fever

IT SEEMED to Eleanor that London was like a huge picture book that was made up of streets instead of pages.

Sometimes the places were very beautiful. There were grand palaces, sparkling fountains, and wonderful parks. One, called Hyde Park, was especially lovely.

"Hyde Park?" Running ahead of her parents, Eleanor called back. "That's where Franklin lives. Are we going to visit him today?"

"Oh, no!" both of her parents answered.

"No?" Eleanor waited until her parents caught up with her. "Why not?"

"Franklin lives in the United States and this park is in London," her mother answered.

"Then why do they have the same name?"

"Franklin's father built his beautiful place on the Hudson River near a town, Hyde Park, named after this lovely park in London."

After thinking about this, Eleanor said, "It's the same as your naming Elliott after Papa."

"You and I have the same name, too, Anna Eleanor, but we decided to call you Eleanor."

"When I grow up, I'm going to name one of my little boys Elliott after Papa, and another one after my husband," Eleanor went on. "When I have a little girl, I'm going to name her Anna Eleanor, after you and me. I guess I'll have to have a lot of children."

Sometimes the places had funny names. There was a big open-air market called Petticoat Lane. There was a tall tower with a clock that had hands fourteen feet long, and the huge bell which struck the hours was called "Big Ben." All the large houses had stables behind them and little streets called mews.

There was a bank which Eleanor's father said was the most important bank in the whole world, but the people of London called it "The Old Lady of Threadneedle Street." There was a place called Piccadilly Circus, but all you could see there were a number of streets coming together, and there was no circus at all.

The policemen were called bobbies, and the guards, in front of the important buildings, stood stiff and straight, like wooden soldiers. Even their eyes didn't move. Suddenly *snap*, the guards came to life, marched a few paces, turned around, and marched back to their posts again. Then *click*, once more they turned back into wooden soldiers.

One day Eleanor and her parents walked

across London Bridge, and later they saw some children playing in a park.

"Oh, look!" Eleanor ran toward them. "They're playing London Bridge, just the way we played it at my birthday party."

When they got closer, however, they discovered that the two children who were standing with their hands joined together high above their heads weren't making a bridge. They were making a bell tower. They were singing a different song, too, as they walked around and around. It was a song Eleanor had never heard before.

> Gay go up and gay go down
> To ring the bells of London Town.
>
> Some are loud and some are soft.
> To play them you must climb aloft.
>
> All the people love to hear
> The bells that ring in London.
>
> Brick-bats and tiles,
> Chime the bells of St. Giles'.

Oranges and lemons,
Toll the bells of St. Clement's.

Pancakes and fritters,
Say the bells of St. Peter's.

Two sticks and an apple,
Say the bells of Whitechapel.

Pokers and tongs,
Say the bells of St. John's.

Kettles and pans,
Say the bells at St. Ann's.

Gay go up and gay go down
To ring the bells of London Town.

One day, when they passed a large church,
Mr. Roosevelt looked up at the high tower and
said, "This is the Church of St. Clement's. I
wonder if the bells really say 'Oranges and
lemons.'"

"Oh, Papa!" Eleanor became very excited.
"Let's stay here until they ring. Then we'll know
whether they really do."

"I've no idea when they might ring," Mr. Roosevelt answered. "We might have to wait a long, long time."

"Couldn't we ask someone?"

"Well, I suppose we could. I'll try to find someone." Mr. Roosevelt started toward a small door. "You wait here and——"

"Oh, no, Papa! I'll come with you." She ran ahead and opened the little door. "I want to see what's on the other side."

The door opened into a small room and there, sitting at a table, was a tall, thin man. He had a long, pointed face and he wore his spectacles on the tip of his nose. Eleanor expected them to slip over the edge any minute and fall down onto his upper lip. "Then he'd look as if he were wearing a mustache, just like Papa," she thought, "only his would be glass."

"Come in! Come in!" The spectacles didn't move. "Pleased to see you. Very pleased to see

40

you." He stood up. "What can I do for you? What can I do for you?"

When he stood up, he looked very odd, like the thin man in the circus. Then, when he said everything twice, Eleanor had to put her hand over her mouth to keep from laughing.

Looking up, she saw that the corners of her father's mouth were twitching, too, beneath his mustache. "I wish I had a mustache to cover my smiling," she said to herself.

Now it was even harder not to laugh. She could imagine the three of them, all with mustaches. Her father would have his dark brown one, and she, a little girl, would have a mustache, too. Then—plop!—the tall, thin man's spectacles would fall off the end of his nose, and he, too, would have a mustache made of two pieces of glass.

Eleanor put her fist in her mouth and held her breath. Her throat felt as if it were filled with

41

a big bubble that was about to burst. She tried to swallow, but she couldn't. "Oh, dear," she thought. "Laughs are harder to swallow than pills." She tried to cough, but that didn't help either. She bit her fist until her fingers began to hurt and then she was able to breathe again.

"It's about the bells," Eleanor heard her father say. "We are looking for someone who can tell us when the bells will ring again."

"Well, you've come to the right place—the right place." The thin man gave a little bow. "I've been the bell ringer here for forty years— forty years. And when will they ring again?" He took a big, round gold watch out of his pocket. "When will they ring again?" He opened the case and looked at his watch over the top of his spectacles. "In twenty minutes. Come back here in twenty minutes and you can watch me ring them—ring them."

When Eleanor and her father returned, the

bell ringer was waiting for them. Looking down at Eleanor, he said, "Would you like to help me ring the bells—ring the bells?" Then he took her hands and put them around the rope.

The end of the rope was some distance from the floor, so Eleanor had to stretch her hands high above her head in order to reach it.

"Now hold on tight! Tight! You mustn't let go for a second—not a single second. Do you promise? Promise?"

Eleanor nodded. Then the bell ringer reached up so that his hands were also high above his head and he, too, took hold of the rope.

Down he pulled, and the rope curled and twisted around Eleanor's shoulders like a huge brown snake. Then up and up it went until, once more, it was stretched out high above their heads. Up and up and up.

Suddenly Eleanor felt her feet leave the floor. She was so surprised she almost let go of the

rope, but she knew, at once, that now she should hold on more tightly than ever. Up and up and up. Then down and down and down. Finally she could feel the cold stone floor beneath her feet once more, but before she had a chance to catch her breath, she was on her way up again.

Up and down, up and down she went, while above her head the big bells rang out loud and clear. They filled the church with their ringing.

Suddenly Eleanor remembered why she was there. Were the bells really saying "Oranges and lemons?" It was easy to pretend they were.

"Oranges and lemons. Oranges and lemons," Eleanor said to herself. After a few minutes the bells began to sound like the market women who called out their wares in Petticoat Lane.

Oranges and lem——

The bell ringer let go of the rope and gave her a little push. Now she felt as if she were flying through the air. She flew past all the people in the stained glass windows. She felt like an angel with wings. Back and forth—back and forth—back and forth. Finally her feet touched the ground again.

"Oh, it was wonderful! Wonderful!" Eleanor looked first at the bell ringer and then at her father. "And I wasn't afraid," she added. "I wasn't afraid." As she said the last words, Eleanor realized that she, too, was repeating everything she said.

"I know you weren't," her father answered quickly. "I know you weren't." Once more Eleanor could see the corners of his mouth twitching beneath his mustache.

Sometimes the people looked strange and exciting. They saw men from Scotland who wore plaid skirts, which Eleanor's father said were called kilts. They saw women from India dressed in yards and yards of beautiful cloth which her mother said were called saris. In one large building they saw some English judges who wore long black robes and long white wigs that reached to their shoulders.

One day they went to the Tower of London and saw the Crown Jewels which belonged to the Queen of England, Queen Victoria. Here the guards were dressed in red and gold uniforms with white ruffs around their necks and roseates on their shoes. They had the strangest name of all—they were called Beefeaters.

One day they saw the changing of the guard at Buckingham Palace. Here the guards wore scarlet tunics, blue trousers, and large bearskin hats, called busbies. Eleanor thought the busbies looked like big, furry animals.

"I wish I could see the Queen," Eleanor stood up on tiptoes and looked at the palace. "Do you think she might come out?"

"I doubt it. Queen Victoria is quite old,"

Mrs. Roosevelt said. "She seldom goes out."

"Couldn't we go in and see her?"

Mrs. Roosevelt smiled. "I'm afraid not."

"Why not?"

"You have to be invited, and only very special people get invitations from the Queen."

Eleanor's mother and father didn't get an invitation from the Queen, but they got invitations from many other people in London. Every evening Eleanor watched while her mother put on one of her beautiful dresses and got ready to go to the opera, the theater, or to a special dinner party. Then, after Mr. and Mrs. Roosevelt left for the evening, Nancy came in and stayed with Eleanor and Elliott.

One evening Eleanor climbed up on the window seat in her bedroom and looked down at the street below.

"Oh, Nancy," she said, "don't you just love being in London?"

"No, I do not!" Nancy was getting Elliott ready for bed while she talked. "I want to go back to New York. I'm homesick."

"Why, Nancy!" Eleanor looked very solemn. "Yesterday Papa said I was just like him. He said I had travel fever. I have travel fever, and you are homesick."

Nancy laughed. "Well, different people get different diseases," she said. "That's just the way it is."

"Oh, come and look, Nancy." Eleanor stood up on the window seat. "The lamplighter is coming down the street. He's almost in front of our hotel right now."

Nancy walked across the room and looked over Eleanor's shoulder. "Humph! I didn't have to come all the way across the ocean to see a lamplighter," she said. "I could see plenty of lamplighters in New York. Besides, the fog is so thick here you can scarcely see."

"Oh, I like the fog." Eleanor pressed her nose against the window. "It makes everything look so—so exciting."

"Well, I don't." Nancy went back to take care of Elliott. "I could do with a bit of sunshine myself. Maybe if the sun would shine for a while it would cure my homesickness."

Eleanor held up her arms. "If you kiss me good-night, Nancy," she said, "maybe you'll catch my travel fever."

Nancy bent down and kissed her. "What if you catch my homesickness?" she asked.

"I'm not afraid of catching it," Eleanor looked at Nancy and smiled. Then, climbing into bed, she pulled the covers up around her shoulders. "I don't think anything will ever cure my travel fever," she added. "I think I'll have travel fever forever and ever."

The Map

WHEN THE ROOSEVELTS had been in London for a month, Eleanor's father got out his big map.

"See," he said to Eleanor, "this is England, where we are now." He pointed to a place on the map that was painted green.

"Tomorrow we are going to take a boat across the English Channel. The English Channel is a broad stream of water between England and France." He moved his finger across a place on the map that was painted blue. "Then, after we cross the Channel, we will visit France." This time he pointed to a country that was pink.

When they arrived at the English Channel

the next day, the water was dark blue and very choppy. The boat they were on bobbed up and down in the waves.

Some of the passengers were seasick. Many people went below, because it was cold and windy on the open decks.

"Come, Little Nell." Mr. Roosevelt held out his hand. "Let's go below where we'll be more comfortable."

"No!" Eleanor held onto the rail of the top deck with both hands.

"Aren't you cold?" Mr. Roosevelt turned up the collar of his overcoat. "I am."

Eleanor nodded, but she held onto the railing more tightly than before. "I want to see France. How long will it be before we get there?" she asked impatiently.

"Why are you so eager to see France?" her father asked.

"Because."

"Because why?"

"Just because."

The boat continued to ride up and down on the waves. Sometimes it seemed as if it wasn't going forward at all. Sometimes it seemed as if the waves were pushing it backward instead. Sometimes it seemed as if it was merely bobbing up and down in one place. Then, at last, a bit of land came into sight.

"There it is." Mr. Roosevelt pointed straight ahead. "There's France. You can see it now."

Eleanor looked at it for a few minutes. Then her eyes began to fill with tears. "That's not France!" she said. "It's not! It's not! I know it isn't France."

"Why isn't it France?" Mr. Roosevelt asked. "What's the matter? Why are you so upset?"

"It can't be France. It can't. It can't." Now tears were rolling down her cheeks.

Mr. Roosevelt stooped down and put his arms

around her. "What's the matter?" he asked. "Tell me why you are crying."

"I—I want to see the map again," Eleanor answered, sobbing.

"The map?" Mr. Roosevelt looked puzzled. "What map?"

"The map you showed me yesterday when we were in London."

Mr. Roosevelt reached into his coat pocket for the map. He handed it to Eleanor.

"See!" Eleanor unfolded it and spread it out on the deck. Then she pointed to the Atlantic Ocean. "See," she repeated, "the ocean is painted blue, and it is blue. England is painted green, and it is green. The trees and the grass and the bushes are all green, just as they are at home. The English Channel is painted blue, and it is blue." She looked out over the water that surrounded their boat.

Then, pointing to France, she said, "See,

France is painted pink. I thought everything that was green in England would be pink in France. I thought the trees and the grass and the bushes would all be pink. I—I could hardly wait to see the pink grass. That's why I wanted to stay up here on the top deck. I thought pink grass would look so pretty. I thought it would look so pretty with the blue water."

Eleanor stared at the French coastline which, by now, was quite close. "Now just look!" she said. "Everything in France is green, just as it is in England and America." She glanced down at the map again and pointed to Italy. "Isn't Italy yellow either?" she asked.

Mr. Roosevelt shook his head. "I'm afraid not," he said.

"Then it's a silly old map." Eleanor pushed it aside with her foot. "It's a silly old map, and it doesn't tell the truth."

Mr. Roosevelt tried not to smile. "The countries are painted different colors on a map so we can see their shapes more easily."

Then he picked up the map, folded it, and put it back in his pocket. "There will be pink blossoms on the fruit trees in France," he said. "Then, when the blossoms fall, the ground beneath the trees will be pink, too. There will be pink flowers along the streets, and in the window boxes, and in the parks. There will even be pink clouds in the sky. So, you see, the map isn't all wrong."

There were pink blossoms on the trees and on the ground below. There were pink flowers along the streets, in the window boxes, and in the parks. There were pink clouds in the sky.

France was so beautiful it cured Nancy of her homesickness. It was so beautiful it made Eleanor's travel fever go higher and higher. Mr. Roosevelt was right. The map wasn't all wrong after all.

Pietro's Shoes

AFTER A MONTH in France the Roosevelts went to a town in Italy called Sorrento. Below the town there was a beautiful sea. Above the town there were beautiful mountains. One day, when Eleanor came out of the hotel, she saw a boy and a donkey standing beside the gate.

"This is Pietro," Mr. Roosevelt said, introducing her to the boy, "and this is his donkey. They will come every day and take you for a ride. However, these mountain roads are rough and dangerous. Whenever you ride, Pietro is to go with you and lead the donkey."

Eleanor was delighted. Every morning, after

breakfast, she and Pietro and the donkey went up into the mountains.

One morning, as Mr. Roosevelt lifted Eleanor onto the donkey's back, he said, "Don't go far today. We might have a storm."

"Oh, no, *Signore.*" Pietro shook his head. "We will not go far. Do not worry. I will take good care of the little *signorina.*"

An hour passed. The gray clouds that hovered over the top of the mountains grew darker and darker. Lightning flashed between the peaks. Thunder echoed and re-echoed in the valleys. Big drops of rain began to fall.

Mr. Roosevelt walked back and forth in front of the hotel. Where were Eleanor and Pietro and the donkey? What had happened to them? Why weren't they back at the hotel?

Mr. Roosevelt was frightened. He knew Pietro would never do anything foolish. The boy had promised that he and Eleanor would not stay long. Mr. Roosevelt knew that Pietro could be trusted to keep his promise.

Suddenly a bright flash of lightning lit up one side of the mountain, and Mr. Roosevelt was able to see to the far end of one of the paths. A second later it was dark again.

He started up the path. He was sure he had seen a donkey and two small figures—one riding on the donkey's back and the other one walking beside the donkey—coming down the side of the mountain.

A moment later he was able to see them quite plainly. Then he realized that something was wrong. Pietro was riding the donkey, and Eleanor was walking beside them, holding the reins.

"Eleanor! Pietro! What happened?" Mr. Roosevelt hurried to meet them.

"Papa!" Eleanor started to run, but the donkey continued his leisurely pace, and Eleanor knew that she had to stay with him.

"Oh, *Signore!*" Pietro began to slide off the donkey's back. "*Signore!*" He ran down the path. He was breathless so that he could scarcely speak when he reached Mr. Roosevelt. "Believe me—it was not my fault. Truly it was not my fault."

He took a deep breath. "I was leading the donkey as you told me and then—then—I stepped on a sharp stone and cut my foot. It happens all the time, *Signore*. Every day! It was nothing. Nothing! But the little *signorina*— she was very upset. She got off the donkey. Then she said, because my foot was bleeding, I should ride and she would walk.

"Of course I refused, *Signore*. I told her it was nothing, that it happened every day. But she would not listen. She stamped her foot. She said 'No! No! No.' Finally she sat down in the middle of the road and would not move.

"I tried to lift her, *Signore*, but as you see, I am not very big. Without her help it was impossible for me to put her on the donkey.

"I waited and waited. 'Soon,' I said to myself, 'she will become tired of sitting there in the middle of the road.' But she just sat there, *Signore*, and did not move.

61

"When it began to storm I said to myself, 'Now she will be frightened. Now she will let me help her back on the donkey, so we can return to the hotel.'

"I think she was frightened, *Signore*. The lightning was very close and the thunder roared all around us. But she didn't move, *Signore*. She just sat there in the middle of the road, as if she were a—rock.

"As the storm grew worse I knew we would have to return to the hotel, but I knew she would not move until I climbed onto the donkey's back. What could I do, *Signore?*" Pietro shrugged his shoulders. "What could I do?"

He paused for a moment. Then he went on. "*Signore.*" He spoke very slowly. "*Signore*, in Italy we say that it is impossible to find anything more stubborn than a donkey. Now—to-day—I know this is not true. Please, *Signore*, I am sorry to say this, but in all my life I have never seen a donkey half so stubborn as the little *signorina.*"

"Papa." By this time Eleanor and the donkey had reached them. "Papa! Look at Pietro's foot. He cut it on a rock and it's bleeding. He should have some shoes to wear. Then the rocks wouldn't cut his feet. Will you buy some shoes for him, Papa? Will you?"

"Please, *Signore*—" Pietro didn't know what to say. "I do not need the shoes. The little *signorina* is very kind, but my donkey and I— we are used to the rocks and the stones. We do not need the shoes."

"Papa!" Eleanor pulled at her father's coat. "The donkey's feet aren't bleeding, but Pietro's are. He should have some shoes. You will get some for him, won't you, Papa?"

Mr. Roosevelt turned to Pietro. "As you know," he said, "she can be more stubborn than any donkey. If she thinks you should have a pair of shoes, I'm afraid there isn't anything either you or I can do about it."

Mr. Roosevelt gave some money to Pietro. "Go buy yourself some shoes. There will be no peace around here until you do."

Pietro looked at the money and put it in his pocket. He looked up at Mr. Roosevelt. "Thank you very much, *Signore*. With this I can buy the best shoes in Sorrento."

Then he looked at Eleanor. "It is true," he said, "that you are more stubborn than a donkey, but you are kinder than anyone I have ever known. I have been a donkey boy for many years, but you are the only person who has ever noticed that sometimes the rocks cut my feet."

Eleanor was up early the next morning. She was eager to see Pietro's new shoes. As soon as she finished her breakfast, she ran down the path to the gate. There, as always, Pietro and his donkey were waiting for her.

"Pietro!" She looked down at his feet. "Pietro! Why didn't you buy some shoes?"

"But I did, *Signorina*. I did!" He looked at her and smiled. "They are the most beautiful shoes in Sorrento."

"But you are barefooted." Eleanor stared at his feet. "Where are they?"

"Where are they?" Pietro shrugged his shoulders. "At home, of course."

"Then why aren't you wearing them?"

"Wearing them? Now? Today?" Pietro looked puzzled. "Oh, *Signorina*, it would be foolish to wear them on these mountain roads."

"But I wanted you to have them so that the rocks wouldn't cut your feet."

"Oh, *Signorina!*" Pietro shook his head. "You do not understand. These are the first shoes I have ever had. They are too beautiful to wear on rough mountain roads. When I cut my foot, it will heal. See!" He held up one bare foot.

"Today it does not bleed any more. By next week even the scar will be gone. But when the shoes are cut they do not heal. They are ruined. If I wore them every day they would be gone in two weeks, cut to shreds by the rocks. Then I would not have my beautiful shoes any more."

"But Pietro! Pietro! Aren't you ever going to wear them?"

"Wear them? Of course I am going to wear them. I shall wear them to church always."

"Pietro," Eleanor said. "I want to go back to the hotel and talk to my father."

"Of course, *Signorina*. Of course." Pietro nodded and smiled. "The ride, it can wait—and my donkey and I, we can wait also."

Eleanor walked slowly up the path to the hotel and sat down on one of the stone steps. She knew her father would come outside as soon as he finished his breakfast.

"Little Nell!" Mr. Roosevelt stood on the top

step and looked down at Eleanor. "I thought you had gone for a ride. What's the matter?"

"I don't like Pietro. I never want to ride with him again. Never! Never! Never!"

"You don't like Pietro? Why not?"

"He won't wear his shoes."

"Won't wear his shoes?"

Eleanor nodded. "He bought some shoes with the money you gave him, but now he won't wear them. He says they are too beautiful to wear every day on the mountain roads. He is only going to wear them to church on Sunday. But he doesn't need them in church. The stones on the floor of the church are smooth. He should wear them when he's in the mountains."

She began to cry. "I wanted him to have some shoes so the sharp rocks wouldn't cut his feet and—and—now he's only going to wear them to church on Sunday."

Mr. Roosevelt sat down beside her. "There is

something you must learn, Little Nell." He put his arm around her shoulders.

"What you give people isn't always important. What they do with your gifts may not be important either. The most important thing you can ever give people is the feeling that you care about them—that you are concerned about them—interested in them. Most of all, you must try to understand them. What is important to you may not be important to them.

"The world is filled with people who need help. Sometimes we can help them and sometimes we can't. But if they know we want to help them and are trying to help them, that can often mean more than anything else.

"When I gave Pietro the money for the shoes, and he bought them, they became his shoes. They don't belong to you or to me. They belong to Pietro. You have no right, now, to tell Pietro where or when to wear his shoes.

"Someday," he added, "when Pietro's shoes are worn out, he will probably remember that once upon a time a little girl named Eleanor Roosevelt worried about him and wanted to help him. Then this will seem much more important to him than his beautiful shoes. This, I am sure, is what he will remember."

Mr. Roosevelt stood up, and taking Eleanor's arm pulled her up beside him. "I can see Pietro and his donkey down by the gate," he said. "They are waiting to take you for a ride."

Eleanor started down the path. Then, turning around, she said, "If Pietro cuts his foot today I'm going to make him ride on the donkey again, just as I did yesterday."

Her father laughed. "All right," he said, "but I imagine Pietro is going to be very careful now. I'm sure he will try very hard not to cut his foot again, at least not as long as you are in Sorrento."

I Promise

AFTER TWO MONTHS in Italy, the Roosevelts returned to France. There Mr. Roosevelt became ill and was taken to a hospital.

Eleanor missed her father very much. She tried to play with Elliott, but he was only two years old. He didn't understand the games she wanted to play. Her mother and Nancy were always busy. She had no one to talk with and nothing to do.

One afternoon she felt especially lonely. She walked from room to room, trying to think of something to do.

"I wish something would happen," she said to

herself. "Something—something special, like a picnic—or a birthday party—or a parade."

"Eleanor!" Mrs. Roosevelt called from her bedroom. "Eleanor, come here. I want to tell you something."

Eleanor walked into her mother's room and sat down on a low stool. This was her favorite room in the whole house. There were always fresh flowers in vases on the tables. Her mother's beautiful dresses hung in the closets. Everything always smelled nice and fresh. Everything always looked pretty.

"Eleanor, it's tea time." Mrs. Roosevelt poured a cup of tea for herself and a glass of milk for Eleanor. "I went to the hospital to see your father yesterday and——"

"You saw Papa?" She almost spilled her milk.

"He sent his love to you and——"

"Can't I go to see him, too?"

Her mother shook her head. "Children aren't

allowed in the hospital," she said. "You will have to wait until he comes home."

"When will he be home? Tomorrow?"

Mrs. Roosevelt shook her head. "No, Eleanor. It will be many, many days, I'm afraid. But while I was there we talked about you."

Eleanor sat up very straight. It made her feel important to think that her father and mother talked about her at the hospital.

"We decided," Mrs. Roosevelt went on, "that you should go to school. There is a convent near Paris which has a boarding school. You will be taught to read and write and speak French. You'll have other children to play with, too, so you won't be so lonely."

School! Eleanor had never been to a school. She had never even seen a school.

A little while before, Eleanor had hoped that something exciting would happen, like a picnic or a birthday party or a parade. Was a school as exciting as a picnic or a birthday party or a parade?

The next morning Eleanor and her mother drove to the convent. When the carriage stopped in front of some tall gates Eleanor felt a little frightened. Mrs. Roosevelt rang a little bell that was fastened to one of the posts. Then, a few minutes later, there was a loud click, and the big gates swung open.

"Ah, Madame Roosevelt." A nun in a long black robe and a wide white headdress came toward them. "We have been expecting you and your little daughter."

She looked down at Eleanor. "I hope you will—" She hesitated a moment as if groping for words. "I hope you will be very happy here. We——" She hesitated again. "We do not speak the English very well, but soon you will be learning the French. It will not take long."

Eleanor looked around her.

Several little girls were sitting on the grass eating fruit, as if at a picnic. Other little girls were playing games. They were singing and holding hands and walking round and round in a big circle. They were having fun as at a birthday party.

Then a bell rang and the little girls formed two straight lines along the walk. They were all dressed alike in dark blue jumpers and white blouses. When the bell rang again they began to march, two by two, into the building. It was even like a parade.

That night, after it grew dark, everything seemed different. The school didn't seem as exciting as a picnic, a birthday party, or a parade. It didn't seem exciting at all.

After supper a nun showed Eleanor where she was to sleep. It was a large room with twelve little beds. "See, Eleanor," the nun said, "you will have eleven roommates—eleven little girls to—how do you say it in English? Ah, yes, now I remember. You will have eleven little girls to keep you company."

Eleanor thought about her new uniform, which was hanging in her closet. One of the nuns had brought it to her just before bedtime.

She missed her father. She missed her mother and little brother. She wanted to be home with them. She didn't want to be in this strange place where she didn't know anyone.

None of the little girls spoke English, and Eleanor couldn't speak a word of French. They all stared at her as if she were an odd kind of person from another world.

Eleanor thought about her new uniform which was hanging in her closet. One of the nuns had brought it to her just before bedtime.

"Perhaps," she said to herself, "when I put it on tomorrow and am dressed like the other children, they won't think I'm so strange."

The new uniform didn't help, however. Even though she was dressed like the other children, she still couldn't understand them, and they couldn't understand her. They played games she had never played, and no one could tell her the rules or how to play them.

When they went into a classroom, a nun would talk for a while to the other children. Then, turning to Eleanor, she would point to some object in the room and tell her what it was called in French. "Repeat after me, please. In French, please." Again the nun would pronounce the word very slowly and carefully.

Eleanor tried to say the words exactly the way the nuns said them, but the French words were difficult to pronounce. Some words had sounds she had never heard before. When she tried to say them, they didn't sound the way she expected them to sound.

This was bad enough, but every time she tried

to say a word in French the other little girls laughed and giggled. Then the nun would talk to them in French. Eleanor couldn't understand what the nun was saying, but she could tell that the nun was scolding.

The scoldings didn't seem to help, however. The next time Eleanor tried to say something in French, all the girls laughed and giggled again. They laughed and giggled when she spoke English, too. They thought everything she did and said was funny.

Eleanor wanted to like the school, but, as the days passed, she became more and more lonely. The nuns, who could speak English, were always busy. She had no one to talk with and no one to play with.

The days seemed endless. They were always the same. Nothing special ever happened. Then, one day, something special did happen.

Madeline, the little girl who slept in the bed

next to Eleanor's, swallowed a penny. Everyone was excited. All the nuns came running and gathered around her. They looked worried and frightened. They felt her head and her stomach. They thumped her on the back. They told her to cough and stick out her tongue. Finally a servant was sent to get a doctor.

The other children stood up in their beds and tried to see what was happening. They were frightened, too. Some began to cry. Some jumped up and down in order to see better. Some ran and stood behind the nuns, peering first on one side and then on the other.

Soon the doctor came, carrying a little black bag. Now there was more confusion than before. Poor Madeline. Everyone was worried about her. Swallowing a penny was an alarming thing to do. It was frightening and terrible and —and—and—wonderfully exciting.

Eleanor's bed was so close to Madeline's that

she could easily see what was happening. "Madeline must feel like a piggy bank with a penny in her stomach," she said to herself, and she didn't know whether to laugh or cry.

The doctor closed his little black bag. He stood up and shrugged his shoulders. He didn't seem to think there was any danger.

After he left, the nuns went from bed to bed. They tried to quiet the little girls. They tucked the blankets around the children and told them to forget the excitement and go to sleep.

The excitement continued. After the doctor left, after the little girls were tucked into bed, after the candles were blown out, after the nuns were gone, the excitement still could be felt. It was a long time before all the children went to sleep.

The next morning Madeline was still the center of attraction. How did she feel? Was she a little pale? Did she have any pains?

Eleanor stood off by herself. No one paid any attention to her. The children acted as if they didn't see her, as if she weren't there. As the day passed she felt more lonely than ever. She wished something exciting would happen to her.

"If I swallowed a penny," Eleanor thought wistfully, "everyone would crowd around me the way they do around Madeline."

All day she thought about how important Madeline had become because she had swallowed the penny. Eleanor could see herself in Madeline's place, the center of attention.

That evening she went up to one of the nuns and said, "I have swallowed a penny."

"Eleanor! Are you sure?"

Eleanor nodded.

"When did you swallow it?"

"A—a—a little while ago."

"But when, exactly?"

"A—a little while ago. I don't know exactly."

"Where did you get the penny?"

"I—well——" Eleanor looked up at the nun and smiled. "My father gave it to me."

"Where were you when you swallowed it?"

"In my—in the—in the garden."

The nun looked very stern. "Eleanor," she said, "I don't believe you swallowed a penny. Now tell me the truth. Did you really and truly swallow a penny?"

Eleanor looked down and nodded.

"Eleanor, look at me." The nun put her hand under Eleanor's chin and made her raise her head. "Look at me and tell me the truth."

Eleanor began to cry. "I did! I did!"

The nun called the other nuns and soon they were all gathered around her. They asked her the same questions over and over again.

Eleanor cried harder and harder, and her one answer to all their questions was, "I did! I did! I did swallow a penny."

One of the nuns said, "We must send for her mother," and all the other nuns agreed.

Still crying, Eleanor was put to bed. The other little girls stared at her, but they did not crowd around her as they had crowded around

Madeline. Instead they whispered to each other in French, and they laughed and giggled.

Eleanor couldn't understand what they were saying, but she was sure they were talking about her. She was sure they were making fun of her, too. Finally she cried herself to sleep.

Mrs. Roosevelt arrived the next day. When she talked to Eleanor she looked as stern as the nuns. "No one believes that you swallowed a penny," she said. "Please tell me the truth. Did you, or didn't you?"

Eleanor looked down at the floor. "I did! I did!" she repeated over and over again.

The nuns were very upset. Finally one of them went up to Mrs. Roosevelt and said, "Eleanor does not seem happy here. Perhaps it would be better if she went home with you."

On the way back to Paris Eleanor sat in one corner of the carriage and twisted her wet handkerchief. Finally she spoke. "Mama!"

"Yes, Eleanor?"

"Mama, I didn't really swallow a penny."

"Oh, Eleanor!" Her mother began to cry, too. "Everyone knew you didn't. Why did you say you did? You know it's wrong to tell a lie!"

Eleanor nodded. She knew it was wrong to tell a lie. She knew, too, that she had never been so miserable in her life. She was sure she would never be happy again as long as she lived.

A few days after she came home her father returned from the hospital. This was wonderful, but shortly after that, another exciting thing happened. Eleanor had a new little brother.

"We've decided to name him Hall," her father told her. "That was your mother's name before she was married."

Eleanor looked at her baby brother. He was so small. He wasn't much bigger than one of her dolls. She had thought Elliott was small. Now he looked large beside this new little baby.

"I'm going to name one of my little boys Roosevelt," she said finally. "Then he'll have my name just as Hall has Mama's."

Mr. Roosevelt laughed. "You said you were going to name one of your boys Elliott, and you want to name a girl Anna Eleanor, so she would have the same name as you and your mother. Then you decided to name another boy after your husband. Now you're going to name one Roosevelt, too. You really will have to have a number of children to use up all those names."

Eleanor nodded. "Yes," she said, "I will have to have a lot of children."

"Well, I think that's a good idea," her father answered, "but there is one thing you must promise. You must promise to teach your children never to swallow pennies. Swallowing pennies makes children very unhappy."

Eleanor looked at her father. She knew he was teasing her. She knew, too, that this was his way of telling her that it was foolish to tell a lie—that just as a penny could make one sick, a lie could make one unhappy.

"I promise," she said. She was sure her father knew that she was really promising to try hard always to tell the truth.

When Eleanor left the convent she thought she had disgraced herself and her family. Now, with her new promise and her new little brother, she was beginning to feel happy again.

As always her father seemed to understand how she felt. "A good, happy feeling inside you is better than a penny, isn't it, Little Nell?"

Eleanor hadn't smiled since she left the convent. Now she threw back her head and laughed. "Oh, Papa," she said, "I—I——"

Her father took her hand. "Hall is crying," he said. "Let's see what he wants. You know you are going to have to help take care of this new little brother of yours."

Surprising
Things Can
Happen

I<small>T</small> <small>WAS</small> T<small>HANKSGIVING</small> morning, and the Roosevelts were back in New York City. Eleanor was sitting on a high stool in the kitchen, and she had a big apron tied around her.

"Now!" she said to the cook as she smoothed the folds of the apron. "You said I could help. What can I do?"

"Well, Miss Eleanor, you may cut up the parsley." The cook brought a large bowl of parsley and the kitchen scissors. "But you must cut it very fine. It's for the turkey dressing."

Eleanor picked up the shears. They were too large and heavy for her small fingers. She tried and tried to use them, but she couldn't make them work. "If I tell the cook I can't use them," she said to herself, "she'll say I'm too little to help, and I do want to help."

Finally she slipped from the stool. "Excuse me," she said. "I'll be back right away."

"Young ones always want to help until you give them a job," the cook said to herself. "Then they find out it isn't as much fun as they thought it was going to be. I'll not see her again until she's eating the turkey and dressing at dinner this evening."

A few minutes later Eleanor was back. "I brought my own scissors," she said, holding up a small pair with blunt edges. "They're the ones I use to cut out my paper dolls, but I think they will cut the parsley, too."

Eleanor climbed up on the high stool again. She picked up a sprig of parsley and snipped and snipped. The small scissors worked fine.

They were just the right size for her little fingers. Snip! Snip! Finally the big bowl was filled with tiny pieces of minced parsley.

"Why, Miss Eleanor!" The cook looked surprised and pleased. "You've been a big help. It would have taken me a long time to do that."

Eleanor was ready to ask for another job when her father appeared in the doorway. "Want to come with me, Little Nell?" he asked.

"Oh, yes, Papa!" She was down off the stool before she said the last word.

"Now, that's not fair, Mr. Roosevelt!" The cook tried to look angry. "You're taking away one of my best helpers."

Mr. Roosevelt laughed. "I'm sorry," he said, "but I need her help, too. I'm afraid you will just have to get along without her."

Eleanor looked from one to the other. She would rather help than do anything else, and here were two people who wanted her to help them. Standing there in the middle of the kitchen, she felt wonderfully happy.

"We'll be home in time for dinner this evening," he called as they left the kitchen. Then, turning to Eleanor, he said, "Go upstairs and put on a warm coat and hat. It's cold outside."

When Eleanor came down the stairs a few minutes later, he looked at her closely. "Is that a new coat?" he asked.

Eleanor nodded.

"It's very pretty." He touched the soft fur collar. "But I think Mama will have to send it back to the tailor. Look! He put an extra button at the top on the right side and an extra buttonhole at the bottom on the left side."

Eleanor looked at the row of buttons and buttonholes on her coat. "Oh, Papa!" Her eyes twinkled and she began to laugh. "You know I just buttoned it wrong."

"Really?" Her father looked surprised. "Is

that really what happened? And here I was blaming the tailor."

After they went outside and got into the carriage, Eleanor looked very solemn. Then she said, "Papa, when you tease me, it's fun. I feel gay and happy. When other people tease me I feel unhappy. I want to run away and hide."

Mr. Roosevelt was silent for a while. Then he began to speak very slowly, as if he were thinking of every word. "You know," he said, "all your life you are going to have to live with one person—Eleanor Roosevelt.

"No matter where you go or what you do you can never get away from yourself. If you try hard to be fair and honest, if you try hard to be an interesting person—you will have a fair and honest and interesting person to live with the rest of your life. Try to be the kind of person you want to be. Then, what other people say to you or about you won't really matter."

"I wish I were like Mama," Eleanor said. "Everyone talks about how beautiful she is. I wish I were just a little bit pretty."

"You are much more than a little bit pretty," her father answered. "You have beautiful blonde hair and lovely blue eyes. Do you know that eyes are like windows? We look out at the world through our eyes, but people can look in at us through our eyes, also. Our eyes show what we really feel and think. You have lovely hands, too, that talk almost as much as you."

"Oh, you're just teasing me." Eleanor looked at her hands. "Hands can't say anything."

"That isn't true," her father answered. "Do you know that in some countries people dance with their hands as well as their feet? Each movement of the dancer's hands means something. Your hands can say almost as much as your eyes." He reached over and pulled one of Eleanor's hands out of her little muff.

"You do have lovely hands," he said, "but don't you think they would be much more beautiful if you didn't bite your nails? You have long, strong fingers, but they should be allowed to have strong, well-shaped nails. Try to remember that whenever you start to bite them."

"I will, Papa! I will!" Eleanor put her hand back into her muff so she wouldn't see her short, bitten nails. "I still wish I were pretty," she said. "I—I wish I looked like Mama."

"Have you ever heard the story of the Ugly Duckling?" Mr. Roosevelt asked.

"No." Eleanor shook her head.

"Well," he began, "once upon a time a mother duck sat upon her nest waiting for her eggs to hatch. At last one eggshell after another burst open, all except one, the very largest.

"Finally this shell opened, too. 'Peep! Peep!' said the little one, and crept forth. He was larger than the others, but not very pretty.

94

" 'He's probably a turkey,' said an old duck, who happened to be passing.

" 'Well,' said the mother duck, 'we'll find out tomorrow.' The next morning the mother duck went down to the water with all her little ones. Splash! Splash!

" 'Quack! Quack!' she said, as one duckling after another plunged in and began to swim. The Ugly Duckling swam with the others.

" 'No, he's not a turkey,' said the mother duck. 'Look how well he can use his legs, and how upright he holds himself. On the whole he is quite pretty, if one looks at him rightly.'

"The other ducks didn't think he was pretty, however. Even the other members of the family didn't think he was pretty.

" 'He's too big,' they said. 'He looks odd and different.'

"The ducks teased him. They pushed him and shoved him. They wouldn't let him swim near them. 'You're different,' they said over and over again. 'Go away! Go away!'

"Some time later two wild geese flew over the farmyard. They saw the Ugly Duckling, all by himself, and swam over to him. 'You appear different,' they said, 'but we like you. Will you go with us and become a bird of passage?'

"The Ugly Duckling was pleased. He thought it would be wonderful to see the world.

" 'Oh, yes,' answered the Ugly Duckling. 'I would like to come with you.'

"They had gone only a short distance when two shots whizzed through the air. Bang! Bang! The Ugly Duckling was very frightened. Then, a second later, the wild geese fell down dead into the swamp.

"Now the Ugly Duckling felt sadder than ever. He didn't know how to get back to the farmyard, and he didn't have anyone to tell him what to do or where to go. He stayed in the swamp all winter. He was cold and sad and lonely, but he had no other place to go.

"Spring came. Then, one day three great handsome swans flew down to the lake which was beside the swamp. They were dazzling white. They had long, beautiful necks. They seemed to float upon the water.

" 'I will go to them,' said the Ugly Duckling. 'I know they won't like me, but, no matter what happens, I must go to them.'

"The Ugly Duckling hurried to the lake. Then, as he bent his head down, he saw his own image. And lo! He was no longer a clumsy dark-gray bird, but a beautiful swan.

"Some children were playing beside the lake. 'Look!' one shouted. 'There is a new swan!' Other children came running. They clapped their hands and jumped up and down. 'Look at the new one,' they cried. 'He is the most beautiful of all!' "

As Mr. Roosevelt finished his story the coachman said "Whoa!" and the horses stopped. As Eleanor's father helped her out of the carriage, he said, "There are many kinds of beauty. Beauty means different things to different people. You may be beautiful in different ways."

"Anyway," he said quickly, "we mustn't spend too much time thinking about ourselves. We must think about other people, too."

They walked across the sidewalk and began to climb some stairs. "This is a clubhouse which my father, Theodore Roosevelt, started many years ago. He built it for the newsboys of New York. Many of them are very poor, and he wanted to do something to help them.

"Some of these boys live in little wooden shanties on empty lots. They built these shanties out of old packing boxes. Some of them don't even have shanties to live in. At night they sleep in doorways or in public buildings.

"Yet they work hard and earn their own livings. Some even support a mother and little brothers and sisters.

"Today," he went on, "my brother Teddy and I and some of our friends are giving a Thanksgiving dinner for them."

"Was Uncle Teddy named after Grandpa Roosevelt?" Eleanor asked.

"Yes, my father was Theodore Roosevelt Senior. My brother, who is your Uncle Teddy, is Theodore Roosevelt, Junior."

Eleanor frowned. "Everyone in our family is named after someone else in the family. Some times I get all mixed up."

Her father laughed. "Don't tell anyone," he said, "but sometimes I do, too."

Mr. Roosevelt opened the front door and he and Eleanor walked into a large room. It was filled with long tables and many chairs.

Then another door opened. Suddenly the

room was filled with boys. Their clothes were worn, ragged and patched. Some boys wore coats much too small or much too large.

Mr. Roosevelt looked at them and smiled. They had all dressed up for the party in the only way they could. They had washed their faces and hands, and had combed their hair.

While the boys were finding their places at the table, Mr. Roosevelt led Eleanor into the kitchen. Here two women were filling plates with turkey, dressing, sweet potatoes, and cranberry sauce. Beside the women were ten men. As soon as the plates were filled, the men carried them into the dining room.

"Here." Mr. Roosevelt handed a plate to Eleanor. "Take it to one of the boys. Be careful, now, don't spill it."

Eleanor held the plate with both hands. It was hot, heavy, and hard to balance. After she took a few steps the cranberry sauce slipped to the very edge. She tilted the plate, and the gravy on the other side burned her thumb.

"No matter what happens, I mustn't drop it or spill it," she said to herself.

The hot gravy continued to burn her thumb. It hurt badly and brought tears to her eyes. When she tilted the plate again the cranberry sauce slid dangerously close to the other edge. She wanted to put the plate down and put her thumb into her mouth to cool it.

"But I mustn't!" she said with every step. "I mustn't. I mustn't."

Finally she reached one of the tables. Then, lifting the plate carefully, she put it down in front of one of the newsboys.

The little boy looked at the food. Then looking at Eleanor, he said, "Thank you, Miss."

Eleanor ran back to the kitchen. "Give me another plate, Papa," she said.

She didn't mind that the plate was hot and

heavy. She didn't mind that the cranberry sauce slipped and the gravy burned her thumb. Reaching up for the second plate, she said, "The little boy said 'Thank you.'"

By the time the last boys were served, some had finished. Now Eleanor helped carry big pieces of pumpkin and mincemeat pie into the dining room.

At first the boys were too busy eating to say anything. Finally they began to talk and laugh. By the time the last piece of pie was eaten, they were all singing songs.

When the dinner was over, Eleanor and her father started home again. After riding a few blocks, Eleanor said, "Papa, I'm hungry."

Mr. Roosevelt looked surprised. "That's right," he said. "We were so busy serving the boys we forgot to eat. But it's good for us to be really hungry sometimes, too."

Eleanor thought for a long time. Then she

103

said, "Tomorrow all those boys will be hungry again, and they won't have a good dinner."

"That's true," her father answered. "My friends and I do what we can to help them, but it isn't nearly enough. Perhaps some day someone will find a way to really help those boys and their families and other people like them. Who knows, perhaps when you grow up you'll be able to help find a way."

"Oh, Papa!" Eleanor started to bite her fingernails. Then she remembered her promise and put her hands into her coat pockets.

"Oh, Papa," she exclaimed, "you're teasing me again."

"No, I'm not," her father answered. "Sometimes Ugly Ducklings turn into beautiful swans. Sometimes little girls and boys turn into very important people. Surprising and wonderful things can happen. Don't ever forget what happened to the Ugly Duckling."

The New Schoolroom

ELEANOR sat on the stairway and watched. Something exciting was happening.

A large wagon stood in front of her house. The front door was propped open. Men took chairs and tables and desks off the wagon and carried them up the front steps. Then they carried the tables and desks up to the second floor, and up more steps to the third floor.

Mrs. Roosevelt had decided to turn the third floor of her house into a schoolroom.

Eleanor was delighted. This school wouldn't be like the one she went to in France. She knew the boys and girls who were coming to this school. Their parents were friends of her parents. All the children spoke the same language. They all played the same games.

On the first day of school the teacher came with slates, slate pencils, and a great many books. An hour later twelve boys and girls climbed the steps to the schoolroom.

The teacher called the roll and learned the names of the children. She told them where to sit. She told them what subjects they would study—reading, writing, arithmetic, spelling, and French. Just before they left she gave them a list of spelling words they were to learn for the next day.

Eleanor wrote the words over and over again on her slate. Then she went to her mother's room with the list. "See whether I know them," she said to her mother.

Mrs. Roosevelt gave her the words one after the other. Eleanor knew every one.

"That's fine," her mother said. "When your teacher calls on you tomorrow I'm sure you'll be able to spell all the words correctly."

Eleanor could scarcely wait until the next day. She wanted to show the teacher and the other children that she knew every word.

As soon as roll call was over the next morning, the teacher started the spelling lesson. She called on one boy and gave him two words. He stood up and spelled both of them correctly.

"I hope she calls on me next," Eleanor said to herself. "I hope——"

A door at the end of the room opened. Eleanor looked around. She saw her mother close the door quietly behind her and sit down in a chair at the back of the schoolroom.

Suddenly Eleanor was frightened. "If I miss a word," she thought, "Mama will be ashamed of me." A few minutes before she had wanted the teacher to call on her. Now she didn't.

"Please! Please! Please!" she said over and over again. "Please don't call on me. Please don't call on me."

"Eleanor."

Eleanor was so busy saying "please" to herself she didn't hear the teacher call her name.

"Eleanor!"

At last Eleanor realized that everyone in the room was looking at her. In the back of her mind she realized the teacher had called her name. She started to bite her nails.

"Eleanor!"

Eleanor stood up beside her seat. All the pupils were looking at her. The teacher was looking at her. Worst of all she knew her mother was looking at her.

"Eleanor, will you spell the word 'store'?"

"S—t," she began slowly.

She had scarcely heard the word. All she could think about were all those eyes which were looking at her. She felt as if her mother's eyes were drilling two holes into her back.

"That's right." The teacher tried to help her. "S-t are the first two letters. Now spell the last part of the word—ore."

"Ore." Eleanor repeated what the teacher said. Then she started again. "S-t, s-t-o-a-r."

The teacher looked disappointed. The other pupils laughed.

"O-a-r has the same sound as o-r-e," the teacher explained, "but the word 'store' is spelled s-t-o-r-e."

Eleanor could feel her face turning red. She started to sit down, but the teacher gave her another word.

"Potato."

Once more Eleanor scarcely heard the word. She was surprised to hear herself saying "p-o-t-a" very slowly. Then, confused, and not sure what the word really was, she stopped.

"That's fine," the teacher said. "Now spell the last part of the word, 'to.'"

Eleanor thought for a minute. "T-o-e," she finished quickly.

Once again all the other pupils laughed. Once again the teacher looked disappointed. Her mother looked disappointed. Eleanor wished she could drop through the floor and disappear.

After the spelling lesson the children had arithmetic and French. All the children, except Eleanor, held up their hands, eager to answer questions. Usually she knew the answers, but she didn't want to stand up in front of everyone again. She was afraid if she stood up, she would forget everything she knew.

At last the long morning was over. The other children rushed out of the schoolroom, but Eleanor walked as slowly as possible.

The school was in her home. Her mother had furnished the room and hired the teacher.

Nevertheless, Eleanor seemed to feel more shy and frightened than any of the other children. "I'm the worst pupil in the whole school," she said to herself, "the very worst."

Finally she reached the back of the room where her mother was waiting.

"Eleanor!" Mrs. Roosevelt looked very stern. "You knew all of those words last night. I know you did. Why are you so afraid? You must get over your foolish shyness."

The next morning Eleanor's mother wasn't sitting in the back of the room. This made Eleanor feel better. If she said something wrong, her mother wouldn't know about it.

Eleanor listened carefully to everything the teacher said. Finally she became so interested that she forgot to think of herself.

By the end of the first month, she felt at home in the schoolroom. By the end of the second month, she was at the head of her class.

112

Tivoli on the Hudson

ONE MORNING when the children came to school they were stopped at the front door by a maid.

"There won't be any school today," she said. "Mrs. Roosevelt is very ill. Someone will let you know when you can come back again."

A few days later Mrs. Roosevelt died of diphtheria. Mr. Roosevelt was ill, too, and back in the hospital. The schoolroom on the third floor was never reopened.

Eleanor and her two brothers went to live with their Grandmother Hall, their mother's mother. A few months later Eleanor's brother, Elliott, died of diphtheria, too.

Then, the following year, her father died in a hospital in Virginia. Eleanor greatly missed her mother and brother, but she missed her father most of all. He was the one who could make her laugh and treated her as if she were grown-up. He had always made her feel gay, helpful, and important.

In the summer Eleanor's grandmother lived in a large house near Tivoli, New York. The house was on the Hudson River, not far from Hyde Park, where Franklin Roosevelt lived. Two of Eleanor's aunts and two of her uncles lived with Grandmother Hall, too. In the winter all of them moved to a house in New York City.

Grandmother Hall was very strict. She didn't think girls should go to public school. Eleanor had a French governess who taught her at home. Every morning, when Eleanor went in to see her grandmother, she had to recite a number of verses from the Bible in French.

She went to a dancing class, too. She learned to dance the polka and the waltz. Later she went to a ballet class on Broadway and learned to toe-dance. She also took piano lessons from a music teacher.

Eleanor's two aunts were as beautiful as her mother had been. Eleanor liked to watch them get dressed for parties and dinners, for the opera and the theater.

More than anything else she liked to do things for them. She liked to run errands, deliver messages, and help in any way she could. When her aunts asked her to do something, she was delighted. She was pleased that they thought her old enough to be helpful.

One time her Aunt Pussie was ill with a sore throat. In the middle of the night she called to Eleanor, who was in the next room.

Half-asleep, Eleanor groped her way to the door. Then, feeling her way along the wall of the hall, she came to her aunt's bedroom. Her aunt was very hoarse. She could scarcely speak.

"Eleanor, will you please get some ice for me?" she asked. "Here." There was a scratching sound and suddenly Eleanor saw a little flame above a candle. Now she could see her aunt, who was sitting up in bed.

"Take these with you." Her aunt handed her the candle and a bucket for the ice.

Holding the candle in one hand and the bucket in the other, Eleanor went down one flight of stairs and then another. As she walked down the first stairway the grandfather clock on the landing began to strike. One. Two. Three. Four. Five. Six. Seven. Eight. Nine. Ten. Eleven. Twelve. It was midnight.

The flame of the candle danced, and its shadows danced too. Things that looked small in the daytime became unbelievably large. Things that looked large became small.

116

When Eleanor tripped on the carpet she imagined that someone had grabbed her foot. When she touched a bump on the bannister she imagined that someone had grasped her hand.

She walked along a long dark hallway toward the cellar door. The cellar always was cold and damp and dark. Even in the daytime it looked and felt spooky.

Eleanor turned the knob and opened the door. She felt a rush of cold, damp air. The candle felt it, too. It leaned backward as if it were afraid. It flickered and sputtered.

Eleanor gasped, and the flame bent even lower. She was sure it was going out.

"Oh, no!" she whispered. The flame seemed to feel her words and began to grow stronger. In a moment it was burning brightly.

Eleanor put her foot on the top step. Then she started to take the next step, but before her foot reached it, she drew back.

The cellar was so dark that the candle was of little use. She was afraid to go down there by herself in the middle of the night. She wanted to go back to her aunt's bedroom. The stairs and the darkness seemed endless.

Turning around, she started back. Then, looking down at the bucket, she remembered her aunt's strange voice. She remembered how pale her aunt looked and how hot her hand felt.

"She's counting on me," Eleanor thought. "If I don't get the ice she'll be disappointed. She'll think I'm too little to help."

Taking a deep breath, she began to walk slowly and carefully down the cellar stairs. Finally she reached the bottom. Now she felt the cold stone floor beneath her slippers.

Eleanor knew this part of the cellar very well. It was the room where the supplies were kept. She came here every day with her grandmother.

Every morning her grandmother measured

out the flour and sugar and coffee for the day.
She counted out the apples and potatoes and
onions. She poured spices from one jar and
vinegar from another. Then Elcanor made

many trips up the stairs to take things to the cook in the kitchen.

Now Eleanor couldn't see the barrels or the baskets or the jars. She could only smell what was in them. Smelling all the different odors made her feel better. She felt as if everything in the room was saying "Hello" in its own way.

"Odors are like voices," she thought. "Some are strong, like the vinegar. Some are weak, like the potatoes. Some are gay, like the spices, and some are musical, like the apples."

She hated to leave the storage room. It seemed so warm and friendly, but she still had a long way to go. The next room was the laundry. Here there were no friendly odors.

"If Mrs. Overhalse, who does the laundry were here," Eleanor thought, "there would be the smell of soapsuds and starch. There would be the smell of wood burning in the little stove where she heats her flatirons. There would be the smell of sunshine that seems to cling to the clothes when Mrs. Overhalse brings them in from the clotheslines in the yard."

Mrs. Overhalse was one of Eleanor's favorite people. Eleanor liked to talk with her and hear about her family. She liked to help Mrs. Overhalse with the washing and ironing.

Now, without Mrs. Overhalse and the pleasant laundry odors, everything looked strange and frightening. In the middle of the night the laundry was just a big, dark, silent, musty room. Eleanor shivered.

The rest of the cellar was even colder and damper. It even looked darker.

Here the stone floor was uneven and slippery. Eleanor stumbled and slipped. The little flame wagged and wavered. Sometimes it was no bigger than a flame on the end of a match. Then it would seem to catch its breath and burn brightly for a few minutes.

Finally Eleanor reached the outside door. It was heavy and hard to open. She put the bucket down on the floor. Then she found a flat place for the candlestick. Using both her hands, she tugged and tugged at the knob.

The door screeched and creaked. Then, suddenly it swung open, almost knocking her down.

Now Eleanor knew she would have to go out into the backyard. Her grandmother kept the icebox here because it was close to the icehouse.

By holding the candle over her head, Eleanor could see both the icehouse and the icebox. The icehouse was big and round. In the winter, when the river was frozen, men cut big blocks of ice from the river. Then they packed straw around the blocks of ice and stored them in the icehouse. Stacked together, the large pieces of ice stayed frozen all summer. Then, bit by bit, they were taken out and put into the icebox.

Eleanor walked across the yard and lifted the

lid of the ice chest. She put the candle on one ledge and the bucket on the other. She found the ice pick and chipped the ice. Then she began to fill the bucket.

The ice was so cold her hands became numb. Now and then she stopped to blow on them, trying to warm them. She heard strange sounds in the darkness. The little flame waved back and forth. Her hands began to ache. Finally she could scarcely move her fingers.

At last the bucket was filled. Eleanor put it down on the ground and set the candle beside it. She closed the lid of the chest.

Puff! The candle went out. Had it been blown out by the wind? By something? By someone? The Hall house was close to the Hudson River. It was also close to a large forest.

Eleanor thought of the large footprints she and her brother Hall had seen when they went for a walk that afternoon. They had never seen any like them before. They wondered what kind of animal had made them. Was that strange animal hiding in the darkness now?

Then Eleanor remembered that the week before a house, farther down the Hudson, had been robbed. Later the police found some empty sacks in the forest near the Hall house. Had the thieves come to rob her grandmother's house? Were they watching her?

Eleanor started to run. Then, remembering the bucket, she ran back and picked it up. It was heavy and hit against her legs at every step.

Soon her heart was beating so fast she could scarcely breathe. Her legs felt so weak she was sure she would never reach the door.

Snap! A twig broke beneath her feet. "Oh!" She wanted to scream, but the "Oh" was only a faint whisper. She tripped on a stone and stumbled. The ice in the bucket clattered. She knew, if she fell, that she would never have the strength to get up again. Finally she reached the door. The iron knob felt like a friendly hand reaching out to save her.

"Now!" she whispered, but when she turned the knob the door wouldn't open. She pushed and pulled. She kicked the door with her feet and pounded it with her fists.

Tears began to run down her cheeks. Would she have to stay out in the yard all night? No one knew where she was, except her aunt who was too ill to leave her room.

Eleanor sobbed. She was sure she would have to stay outside all night. Finally she gave a hard push with her shoulder, and the heavy door swung open. Now the dark basement, so frightening before, felt warm and friendly.

She started to feel her way across the dark room. Then she remembered that she had left the ice bucket outside in the yard. Going back, she opened the heavy door once more. Then, keeping it ajar with one foot, she reached out and picked up the bucket.

An owl screeched and a twig snapped. Pulling the heavy bucket inside she slammed the door behind her. Now she had to feel her way, slowly and carefully, back through the cellar and the dark house to her aunt's room.

"Eleanor!" Her aunt was sitting up in bed. "What happened? It took you so long. I was beginning to worry about you."

As Eleanor filled the icepack with ice she told her aunt what had happened.

"Oh, Eleanor!" Her aunt looked distressed. "I'm so sorry. Were you frightened?"

"No." Eleanor shook her head. "I wasn't frightened. I was just afraid."

Her aunt smiled. "Is there a difference?"

"Oh, yes," Eleanor said. "When you're frightened you run away. When you're afraid you keep on doing what you're supposed to do."

A Visit with Uncle Teddy

"How MUCH LONGER will it be?" Hall leaned out of the carriage window and stared ahead.

"I'm not sure." Eleanor knew her brother was as impatient as she. She leaned out of the window on her side of the carriage. "I think we should be there in another hour."

"Another hour!" Hall looked at his sister as if she were to blame for the long ride. "Another hour! We'll just get there in time to turn around and come home."

"Now Hall!" Eleanor had helped take care of her little brother for many years. Sometimes she felt more like his mother than his older

sister. "Why we'll have all afternoon and evening and part of tomorrow."

"That's not nearly long enough," Hall answered, "especially when we are only allowed
to visit Uncle Teddy twice a year. I don't think
it's fair. I think Grandmother Hall should let us
visit him and Aunt Edith more often. After all,
he is our uncle."

"Well, it's a long ride, so whenever we go we
have to stay over night," Eleanor answered.
"You know Grandmother doesn't like for us to
be away from home over night very often."

"I don't think that's the reason," Hall grumbled. "I think she's jealous. I think she's jealous
because she knows we like Uncle Teddy more
than anyone else in the world.

"There's another reason, too," Hall went on.
"I heard Grandmother talking to Aunt Pussie
about it. Grandmother is afraid we're going to
grow up like 'all those Roosevelts.' She said,

'I don't want my daughter's children growing up like all those Roosevelts. I want them to take their place in New York Society.'"

Eleanor laughed. "That's right. Grandmother always says, 'I want you to take your place in Society'—Society spelled with a capital S."

"I don't want to belong to any silly old Society spelled with a capital S," Hall grumbled. "I don't want to be dressed up all the time. I don't want to go to silly teas and grand balls. I want to be like 'all those Roosevelts'."

He looked at his sister. Now he was laughing, too. "After all, we are Roosevelts. I'm Hall Roosevelt and you're Eleanor Roosevelt. Even Grandmother Hall can't change that."

"You must remember that Grandmother is old." Once more Eleanor tried to explain. "She has old-fashioned ideas and she is set in her ways. You must remember, too, that Grandmother has four grown children who are still at home. It wasn't easy for her to take us into her household when we were so young. You were only a baby when we went there. We——"

Eleanor looked out of her window again. "Look, Hall!" she cried. "Look! There's Sagamore Hill. I can even see Uncle Ted's house on the very top. We're closer than I thought."

"Really?" Hall looked out of his window. "Say, you're right. I can even see the water from my side. I can see Oyster Bay."

Hall leaned so far out that Eleanor grabbed his coat. "Hall! Be careful. You know, if you fall out, you'll never get there."

Hall allowed himself to be pulled back. "Boy!" He stretched out his long legs. "Boy! I would rather visit Aunt Edith and Uncle Teddy than anyone else in the world. Wouldn't you?"

Eleanor nodded. "You don't remember Papa," she said, "but Uncle Teddy looks very much like Papa. He even makes me feel gay and happy the way Papa did. She smoothed her hair and straightened her hat. "We're almost there," she said. "Do I look all right?"

Hall scarcely glanced at his sister. "Of course you look all right," he said. "Girls are so silly. They're always saying, 'Do I look all right? Is my hair smooth? Is my hat straight?' Of course you look all right," he repeated. "You look just the way you always do."

"That's just the trouble." Tears came to Eleanor's eyes. "I'm dressed now the same as I was dressed when I was a tiny little girl. I'm not a little girl any more. I'm fourteen years old. Aunt Edith buys Cousin Alice beautiful clothes. Alice is only eight months older than I, but she looks grownup. Aunt Edith lets her dress like a young lady.

"And look at me! Dressed like a little girl! I'm taller than Alice, too. That makes me look even sillier in these clothes." Eleanor looked

131

down at her short skirt, her long black cotton stockings and her high button shoes.

"I suppose there will be a lot of other boys and girls there today, too," she added. "There always are. Alice has so many friends and they're together so often. They always talk about things they've done together or are going to do. I never know what to say."

They went around one bend in the road and another. Then they went up and up and up a long, steep hill. Finally they turned into a stone driveway. Now, in front of them, was their Uncle Teddy's big half-brick, half-frame house. Their uncle was waiting for them.

"Eleanor! Hall!" He ran down the steps and started pulling them out of the carriage as soon as the horses stopped.

He pounded Hall on the back. He gave Eleanor a big bear hug. "Dee-lighted to see you. Dee-lighted." He turned Eleanor around. "How

132

you've grown. You're as tall as I am. My, but it has been a long time since I've seen you."

Taking their arms he hurried them up the front steps. "We've been waiting for you," he went on. "As usual, Alice has the house filled with friends. You know how I feel. I think everyone should get a lot of exercise outdoors. As soon as you're ready, we'll play a game."

Uncle Teddy opened the front door. A loud mixture of talking and laughing could be heard.

"Eleanor! Hall!" Their Aunt Edith was waiting for them in the hallway. She shook hands with Hall. She kissed Eleanor on both cheeks. "How wonderful to see you again."

She led them into the living room. Then Alice hurried over to greet them. "Come in! Come in and meet everyone."

Eleanor saw that the room was filled with young people. About half the boys and girls were related to her in some way. However, since she wasn't allowed to go visiting often, she didn't know any of them very well.

"Oh, dear!" she thought. "Now I'll have to go around the room and say 'How do you do' to all of them." She started to follow Alice across the room. Her cousin looked very stylish and grown-up in a beautiful long dress.

Eleanor looked down at her own short skirt and ugly black stockings. She was sure everyone in the room was looking at her. Did they want to laugh, or did they feel sorry for her? She felt so shy and awkward she was sure she wouldn't be able to say a word. She wished she was back in her grandmother's house.

Her Uncle Teddy seemed to know how she felt. He seemed able to read her mind, just as her father had done. "No time to meet anyone," he said. "We've all been inside too long now. We need exercise and fresh air." He clapped his hands. "Silence, everyone! Silence!"

"We're going to play Follow the Leader," he announced, "and there are only two rules. First, you must follow me, no matter where I go. Second, you must do everything I do. If I run, you must run. If I walk on tiptoes, you must walk on tiptoes. If I jump out of the window, you

135

must jump out of the window. Anyone who can't follow won't get any supper."

Everyone laughed. They were all fond of Alice's father. He could always think of some madcap game for them to play. He took them on all kinds of wild adventures. When they came to his house at Oyster Bay they never knew what was going to happen.

Mr. Roosevelt clapped his hands again. "Line up," he said. "Line up behind me."

There was a great deal of shoving and pushing. Now everyone was talking and laughing again. Finally there was a wiggly line of boys and girls walking toward the door.

Eleanor slipped into line. She was so busy keeping up with the others that she forgot to feel shy. Then she noticed that she was the only one in the room who was wearing a hat.

"Oh, dear," she said. "I wonder what I can do with my hat."

She looked at the boy who was right behind her. He smiled at her and held out his hand.

"Give it to me," he said.

Eleanor pulled out the two big hatpins and took off her hat. She put the pins back in the crown and put it on the boy's outstretched hands as if she were hanging it on a peg.

The boy took the wide straw hat and sent it skimming across the room. It landed on top of a high-backed chair with long, slender arms.

Eleanor and the boy looked at each other and laughed. The chair looked like a thin little lady who had come to tea. She sat up straight, with her arms stretched in front of her, and she wore a big straw hat on her head.

"My grandmother never lets me go out of the house without a hat," Eleanor said, as they followed the line down the steps. "It's fun to be where a chair can wear your hat."

She didn't have time to say anything else.

Uncle Teddy started to run across the lawn and they all had to run fast to keep up with him.

"Following the Leader," they raced up one hill and down another. They fell down and jumped up again. They crossed a little stream on a narrow log. They crossed another stream on slippery stones. They climbed over fences and under fences. They waved and shouted.

For once Eleanor was glad she had on a short dress. Alice, in her long skirt, was having a hard time keeping up with her father.

Finally he led them into a big barn at the end of the farm. They mooed at the cows. They barked at the dog. They neighed at the horses.

Then he led them up a steep ladder to the loft. It was filled, up to their waists, with fresh hay. When they tried to walk through it, they stumbled and fell.

"All right! Here we go!"

Eleanor saw her uncle standing in front of an

open window at the far end of the loft. "Oh, no!" Eleanor stared at him. She saw him stoop down and disappear.

Eleanor knew her uncle had been a weak and sickly child. She knew he had fought his way back to health through vigorous exercise and by playing rough and exciting games. She remembered how he had taught her to swim, and had thrown her into water over her head.

Now he had jumped out of a window from the loft of a barn! Surely even Uncle Teddy wouldn't do anything like that!

Foolish or not, he jumped, and all the boys and girls behind him jumped. One by one they came to the window, stooped down, and jumped. Eleanor couldn't believe her eyes.

A few minutes later Eleanor found herself at the head of the line. She had decided not to jump out the window. She merely wanted to see what had happened to the others.

As she moved forward she sank down in the deep hay. She stumbled and fell. One of her shoes came off. She had to look for a few minutes before she found it.

Finally she, too, was standing in front of the open window. She covered her eyes. She was afraid to look. She was sure she would see her uncle and half the boys and girls lying on the ground. She was sure they would be moaning and groaning, with broken arms and legs.

She took her hands from her eyes and looked. Below her, a little distance from the barn, were her uncle and Alice's friends. They were jumping up and down, shouting and calling to her.

"Jump!" they screamed. "Jump!"

Eleanor looked down. Then she saw, right below her, the highest haystack she had ever seen. It was leaning against the barn as if it were too tall to stand alone.

She wanted to laugh and cry at the same

time. Suddenly everything was all right again. Her uncle hadn't lost his mind after all.

Eleanor stooped down as the others had done. She jumped. Then, delighted and amazed, she slid down the haystack, feet first.

It was wonderful. She could feel the warm sun on her face. She could smell the new-mown hay. The hairpins came out of her blond hair. It trailed behind her like the tail of a comet.

"I feel as if I'm sliding down the side of a rainbow," she said, half-aloud. A moment later she was standing beside the others.

"Jump!" she shouted up to Hall, who had just come up to the window. "Jump!"

Eleanor saw his small, frightened face change. He threw back his head and laughed.

"Jump!" she shouted again. "It's wonderful."

Then, throwing her arms around her uncle, she said, "Everything is wonderful here. I wish I could stay here forever and ever."

—And All Grown-up

ELEANOR stood in front of a mirror in her aunt's room and looked at herself.

"I hate this dress," she said, pulling at the skirt. "I hate all my dresses. I hate going to dances, too. I don't know anyone, and no one ever asks me to dance. I don't blame them. Who would want to dance with a tall, gawky person in an awful dress like this?"

"Now Eleanor!" Aunt Maude tied a ribbon through her niece's hair. "You know your grandmother still thinks of you as a little girl. She doesn't want you to grow up too fast."

"But I'm not a little girl." Tears came to

Eleanor's eyes. "I'm fifteen years old. Grandmother can keep me from looking grown-up, but she can't keep me from growing. I'm much taller than most of the girls."

"Well, your grandmother thinks girls should be dressed according to age instead of size," Aunt Maude explained. "So you might as well stop fussing and get ready to go."

"I wouldn't care so much if she didn't make me go to these dances," Eleanor went on. "Why does she make me go when I hate them so?"

"You know your grandmother thinks every young lady should learn to dance. You've been taking dancing lessons for years. What use are lessons, if you don't go to parties and dance?"

"What is the use of going to dances, if no one asks me to dance?" Eleanor tugged at her skirt again. "Since I'm a wallflower, I might as well stay home. I could read a book at home."

"Now, Eleanor," her Aunt said calmly as she

put on her coat, you know you have to go, and we shouldn't be late."

When they arrived, Eleanor's beautiful aunt was surrounded by admirers. Soon she was on the dance floor, dancing the polka.

Eleanor looked around the large ballroom. One side, lined with chairs, was for the older women, who had come to watch. Young ladies, who didn't have partners, sat there, too. Eleanor walked over to one of the chairs. She felt lonely and left out of all the fun. Then she remembered how she had felt in the French school when she was five years old.

"Perhaps I should tell everyone that I have swallowed a penny," she thought. "I'm sure no one would believe me, any more than they did before. But perhaps Aunt Maude would be so ashamed of me she'd let me go home."

Eleanor saw her cousin Alice dancing with a handsome boy. As they came closer Eleanor

144

recognized her distant cousin, Franklin Roosevelt. "He looks more grown-up," she thought, "than the last time I saw him."

Soon the dance ended. The couples clapped and left the floor. Now Eleanor felt more miserable than ever. She tugged at her skirt. She stared at the chandelier. She looked around at all the pictures on the walls.

Across the dance floor, Franklin was leaving Alice and was walking toward Eleanor's side of the room. Eleanor didn't want him to see her sitting there alone. She pretended to fix the buckle on her dress. If she kept her face bent low enough he might not notice her.

"Hello!" Franklin was standing in front of her. "I haven't seen you for a long time, but I've been hearing things about you. I hear you have a very high-spirited horse that is a good jumper. I hear you ride very well."

Eleanor laughed. "Well, for years the family

has been telling me about that wild ride you gave me when I was two years old. Perhaps that's why I'm so interested in riding."

Franklin sat down beside her. "It's good to see you laugh," he said. "When I came up you were looking so solemn."

"I was lonely," Eleanor explained. "I was almost ready to swallow a penny."

"Swallow a penny?" Franklin looked puzzled.

Eleanor laughed again. Then she told him what had happened at the school in France.

Franklin took two pennies out of his pocket. "Well," he said, "here's one for you and one for me, but I don't think they will taste very good, do you?" Across the room a long table had been set with all kinds of delicious food. "Wait just a minute," he said. "I'll see whether I can't find something better for us to eat."

Eleanor was still sitting on the same chair. She still had on the same clothes. Again she

was alone, yet everything was different. "This is a very nice party," she thought.

When Franklin came back with their plates, they forgot about their food and began to talk. They were still talking when it was time to leave.

As they told each other good-by, Franklin said, "This is the last day of spring vacation. I leave for school tomorrow. It will be three months before I can come back to New York. When I return, I want to see you. I can't tell you how much I've enjoyed talking with you."

However, Eleanor and Franklin did not see each other for a long time. A week after the dance, Eleanor's grandmother said to her, "My child, I have decided that it is time for you to go away to school. More than anything else I want you to have a good education. I know this is what your mother and father wanted, too. I have arranged for you to go to Allenswood, a fine boarding school in England."

"Oh, Grandmother!" Eleanor was surprised and delighted. "Oh, Grandmother, I——"

"You will have to work hard," her grandmother went on. "Sending you to England is expensive. You mustn't waste your time while you are there."

"Oh, I won't, Grandmother. I won't. I'll work hard. I promise."

As her grandmother rose to leave the room, she said, "You will need more clothes to wear at school. Your Aunt Pussie and your Aunt Maude have suits and dresses which they aren't wearing any more. We can have them shortened for you."

After her grandmother left, Eleanor walked back and forth across the room. Everything was happening at once. It all seemed too wonderful to be true. Then, remembering the word shortened, she began to laugh. Her grandmother thought Eleanor was old enough to go away to school—to be sent to England. "But I'll still have to wear short dresses. Grandmother still thinks I'm a little girl."

A month later Eleanor sailed for England with her aunt. After a night in London, they went by carriage to the Allenswood School.

The first girl Eleanor met there was Marjorie Bennett. "I'm going to be your roommate," Marjorie said. "Come, I'll show you our room."

While Eleanor unpacked, Marjorie told her about the school. "There are a great many rules, but there's one that is especially important. Do you speak French?"

"Yes, I do," Eleanor answered.

"Oh, that's wonderful." Marjorie looked pleased. "After the first day of school no one is allowed to speak anything except French. A girl stands by the dining room door as we go in for supper. If we have spoken even one word of English during the day, we are supposed to tell her. Since you come from the United States, I was afraid you might not speak French. I was afraid it would be difficult for us to talk with each other."

Eleanor laughed. "I've had French nurses and French governesses and French tutors all my life," she said. "I speak French almost as easily as I speak English."

Eleanor liked the school very much. For the first time in her life she had friends her own age. She also greatly admired Mademoiselle Souvestre, the head mistress. Mademoiselle Souvestre liked Eleanor, too. Before long Eleanor became one of her favorite pupils.

Often Mademoiselle Souvestre invited a few of her favorite pupils to visit her in the evening. First she would read to them. Then they would talk about the things she had read.

One evening she asked Eleanor to come to see her alone. "Why has she asked me to come alone?" Eleanor wondered. "Have I done something wrong? Is she disappointed in my school work? Has something happened to someone in my family?"

Mademoiselle Souvestre was smiling when she opened the door at Eleanor's knock. "Come in, my dear, and sit down. I want to ask you a question." She offered Eleanor a cup of tea and sat down beside her.

"I want to take a trip during the Easter holidays," she went on. "I want to visit France and Italy. I'd like very much for you to go with me. Would you like to go?"

"Oh, Mademoiselle Souvestre!" Eleanor began to laugh. "When you said you wanted to ask me a question, I was afraid I wouldn't know the answer. Now I'm too excited to say 'Yes'."

"I'm an old woman," Mademoiselle Souvestre continued. "I tire easily. You will have to do my packing and unpacking as well as your own on the trip. You will have to check on trains and boats, buy the tickets, and make reservations. Do you think you can do that?"

Eleanor was very pleased. All her life other people had done these things for her. Now she was going to do them for someone else.

On the first day of spring vacation Eleanor and Mademoiselle Souvestre left for Paris. On their way to the railway station Eleanor checked her tickets carefully. There were train tickets to the English Channel, boat tickets to cross the Channel, and train tickets to Paris.

When they arrived at their hotel in Paris Mademoiselle Souvestre turned to Eleanor and said, "I knew I could depend on you. You took care of everything very well. I can't imagine a better traveling companion."

Later that evening Eleanor started to unpack their luggage. "Eleanor, your clothes don't seem right for you," Mademoiselle Souvestre said as

Eleanor hung her own clothes in a closet. "Did you have them made in New York?"

Eleanor looked at her dresses and sighed. "These clothes used to belong to my aunts," she explained. "My grandmother had them made over for me before I came to England."

Mademoiselle Souvestre nodded. "I thought so," she said. "Now that we are in Paris I think you should have a new dress—a dress made just for you. I know a dressmaker who is not very expensive. We will go there tomorrow."

The next morning Eleanor and Mademoiselle Souvestre went to a little shop which was filled with materials and patterns. "Oh!" Eleanor looked at a bolt of dark red wool. "Oh, Mademoiselle Souvestre, isn't this beautiful?"

Mademoiselle Souvestre looked at the cloth carefully. Then she rubbed it between her fingers. "It is beautiful," she said, "and very fine. It's just right for you."

154

"I'm so glad you think so. I—"

"Perfect!" The dressmaker was as delighted as Eleanor. She unrolled the material and draped it around Eleanor's shoulders.

The dressmaker began to cut and pin the material. In half an hour Eleanor could tell how the dress was going to look.

"Come back in a week." The dressmaker smiled as she waved good-by. "The dress will be finished for you."

When Eleanor returned, her dress was waiting for her. Looking at it, Eleanor could scarcely believe that it belonged to her.

"Come, try it on." The dressmaker seemed as excited as Eleanor. "There!" She helped Eleanor with the belt. "Now!" She led Eleanor to a long mirror. "See!" She looked very pleased. "The dress is nice, yes?"

Eleanor was pleased, too. "Oh, yes. It's lovely." She smiled at the dressmaker. Looking in the mirror, she said, "This is my first long dress. It's also the first dress I've ever had made in Paris. I'm sure I'll never have another one that will please me more."

After a few days in Paris, Mademoiselle Souvestre said, "My dear, I get very tired when I go sight-seeing. However, I want you to see the wonderful cities that we plan to visit—Paris, Rome, and Florence. Take your guidebook and go alone. Each day when you return we will discuss what you have seen."

Eleanor was delighted. She was sixteen and had never been allowed to go anywhere alone. Now Mademoiselle Souvestre considered her old enough to take care of herself. Eleanor visited churches and museums. She bought small gifts for her friends. She walked up and down narrow streets where few tourists ever went. Sometimes she got lost, but she always managed to find her way back to her hotel.

Shortly after Eleanor and Mademoiselle Souvestre returned to Allenswood, some girls rushed into Eleanor's room.

"Look!" One of the girls showed Eleanor a picture in a newspaper. Under the picture it said, "Colonel Theodore Roosevelt, Author and Famous Roughrider, Takes Office as Vice-President of the United States."

"We wondered—" She hesitated. "We wondered whether you are related to him."

Eleanor nodded. "He's my uncle—my father's brother."

"Eleanor!" The girls were really excited. "Why didn't you tell us?"

"I don't know." Eleanor felt bewildered. "I've never been very much interested in politics. I guess I never thought of him as the Vice-President of the United States. I just thought of him as my Uncle Teddy."

The following summer Eleanor visited her

grandmother at Tivoli. Shortly before she returned to England, they learned that President McKinley had been assassinated. Theodore Roosevelt became President.

When Eleanor returned to Allenswood her schoolmates were very excited once again. Now Eleanor's Uncle Teddy was the President of the United States.

"Eleanor!" Her roommate, Marjorie, came up and turned her around to look at her. "You look lovely—and all grown-up. Your uncle must be very proud of you."

Eleanor looked at her and smiled. "I hope so," she said in reply. "I've been proud of him all my life."

Eleanor and Franklin

AFTER THREE YEARS at Allenswood, Eleanor returned to the United States. Then she and her Aunt Pussie decided to live in Grandmother Hall's house in New York City.

Her grandmother still lived at Tivoli, and Eleanor visited her often. One day, when she was on the train going back to New York, she heard her name called.

"Eleanor!"

Looking up, she saw Franklin Roosevelt standing in the aisle.

"Eleanor! I didn't know you were back." Franklin sat down beside her. "You've been away a long time. Did you like the school in England?"

"Oh, it was wonderful. I'll always be grateful to my grandmother for sending me there. During my vacations I was able to travel all over Europe. That was wonderful, too."

"What are you going to do now?" Franklin looked at Eleanor as if he had never seen her before. She looked so grown-up.

"Grandmother Hall and my aunts say I must be introduced to New York Society. My aunt, Mrs. Stanley Mortimer, is giving a theater party and dance for me. I suppose I'll have to spend all my time going to dances and parties."

Franklin laughed. "You make it sound terrible," he said. "I thought girls liked to go to dances and parties."

"Well, I don't." Eleanor looked very serious. "Anyway, I never know what to say to people at parties and dances."

Laughing, she added, "My Aunt Maude told me what to do when I couldn't think of anything to say. She said I should take the alphabet and start right through it. 'A—apple. Do you like apples, Mr. Smith? B—bears. Are you afraid of bears, Mr. Jones? C—cats. What do you think of cats, Mrs. Jellyfish?' "

Franklin laughed too. "I think you will do all right. By the time you get to Z—zebras, the party will probably be over."

"What about you?" Eleanor looked serious again. "What are you doing?"

"I'm a senior at Harvard," Franklin answered. "I'm going to study law."

After Eleanor and Franklin met on the train, they saw each other often. Whenever Franklin could leave school he came to New York and took her to some of the parties and dances.

However, they always talked more than they danced. He told her about the work he was doing at Harvard. She told him about some classes she was teaching at a settlement house.

"I teach dancing to a group of children," Eleanor explained. "They come from very poor families. Some of them don't even have enough to eat. Many of them have to work.

"We give them hot food, and it's wonderful to see how much they enjoy the simple dances we teach them. For most of them it's the only time they ever have any fun."

She looked around the crowded ballroom where they were talking. "It makes all of this seem silly and unimportant," she added. "I'm happier when I'm teaching those children to dance than I am when I'm dancing here."

After Franklin graduated from Harvard, he entered the Columbia Law School. He wanted to be in New York so he could see Eleanor more often. When she had classes at the settlement house, he met her there and took her home.

One day a little girl became ill. A few minutes later Franklin arrived. Eleanor asked him to help her take the child home.

After Franklin saw the terrible slum where the little girl lived, he said, "I didn't know anyone lived like that."

"See," Eleanor answered, "this is what I've been talking about. There are thousands of people who live like this. Something has to be done to help them."

On March 17, 1905, there were big headlines in the New York newspapers:

PRESIDENT THEODORE ROOSEVELT GIVES
AWAY HIS NIECE ELEANOR IN MARRIAGE

ELEANOR ROOSEVELT MARRIES
FRANKLIN DELANO ROOSEVELT

THE PRESIDENT AND HIS WIFE ATTEND
THE ROOSEVELT-ROOSEVELT WEDDING

Eleanor's wedding dress was heavy white satin, with a court train and a trimming of lace. Her rose-point Brussels lace veil had been worn by her Grandmother Hall when she was married. She wore a collar of pearls, a present from Franklin's mother. Her veil was fastened with a diamond pin, once worn by her mother. She carried a bouquet of lilies of the valley.

Eleanor looked very beautiful as she walked down the aisle with her Uncle Teddy, the President of the United States. She was tall and slender. Although she was only twenty she had a quiet dignity few girls her age had.

Her Aunt Edith was especially proud of her. Turning to a friend who was sitting next to her, she said, "How lovely she looks. Our little ugly duckling has turned into a beautiful swan."

That summer Eleanor and Franklin went to Europe. Both of them had traveled a great deal. Both of them spoke a number of languages.

Now, together, they were able to visit many places they had visited before.

In Scotland they visited some old friends. One day these friends said to Eleanor, "Our church is having a bazaar. We hope you will make an opening speech."

"Talk in public!" Eleanor's voice quivered. "Never! I just couldn't."

"Since you are the niece of the President of the United States," her friends went on, "you would add color and importance to the bazaar."

"I'm sorry." Eleanor looked very unhappy. "I've never made a speech in my life. Let Franklin do it instead. I'm sure if I tried to make a speech, I'd die of fright."

The following year their first child was born. They named her Anna Eleanor, after Eleanor and Eleanor's mother.

Their second child was a boy and they named

him James, after Franklin's father. The next boy was named Franklin Delano Roosevelt, Jr. This little boy died when he was eight months old. Their next son was named Elliott, after Eleanor's father.

Four years later they had another son. He, too, was named Franklin Delano Roosevelt, Jr., after his father. In 1916 they had another boy. He was named John, after Franklin's uncle.

When Eleanor was little she had said, "I have so many names I want to use. I guess I'll have to have a lot of children. I'm going to name one of my boys Roosevelt. Then he'll have my name the way Hall has Mama's name."

Eleanor had enough children to use all the names she wanted to use. She didn't have to name one of her sons Roosevelt, because all of them had this name.

After Franklin graduated from law school, he became interested in politics. In 1910 he was elected a state senator, and the Roosevelt family moved to Albany, New York.

When Woodrow Wilson became President of the United States, Franklin was made Assistant Secretary of the Navy. Now the Roosevelt family moved to Washington, D.C.

After the First World War was over, Franklin was sent to Europe to help dispose of naval supplies. Eleanor went with him. Once more they traveled through Europe together, but this time everything looked different.

They visited battlefields and naval stations. They saw thousands of buildings in ruins. They visited army hospitals where the wounded soldiers were being treated.

They returned home on a ship called the "George Washington." President Woodrow Wilson and his wife were passengers, too.

Whenever the Wilsons and the Roosevelts were together they talked about a new organization called The League of Nations. They hoped the countries of the world could work together to prevent future wars.

In 1920 the Democratic Party nominated Franklin Roosevelt for Vice President to run with James M. Cox for President.

Eleanor went with Franklin on one of his campaign trips. She heard him speak to many groups of people. In every speech he talked about The League of Nations. He hoped the people of the United States would join and support this new organization.

James M. Cox and Franklin Roosevelt didn't win the election. Mr. Warren G. Harding became the President of the United States.

Once more the Roosevelts moved back to New York City. Eleanor was busy with her large family. She also went to business school and studied typing and shorthand every day. She took cooking lessons twice a week, too.

The Roosevelts had a summer home on a Canadian island called Campobello. They went there every summer.

In August of 1921, when the Roosevelts were at Campobello, Franklin became seriously ill. His legs became paralyzed, and the doctors decided that he had polio.

Eleanor nursed Franklin for many weeks. A good friend of Franklin's, Louis Howe, came to stay with the Roosevelts. He helped Eleanor in every way he could. Finally they were able to move Franklin to a hospital in New York City.

When Franklin was able to leave the hospital, his mother wanted the family to move to her house at Hyde Park. She was sure her son was going to be an invalid for the rest of his life.

Eleanor and Louis Howe didn't agree with her. They were sure Franklin could continue to lead a useful and interesting life. They often discussed his future.

One day Louis Howe said to Eleanor, "You are the only person who can help your husband. You must become interested in politics, too. You must join organizations and take an active part in them. You must work for the Democratic Party. You must invite important political leaders to your home. If you show interest in politics, Franklin will become interested again.

"Most important of all, you must speak to many different groups and organizations. You must tell them what Franklin told them when he was running for the vice-presidency."

Eleanor was very upset. "You know I will do anything to help Franklin," she said. "I've nursed him and taken care of him. I've encouraged him in every possible way. I'm willing to join organizations. I'm willing to work for the Democratic Party. But I could never make a speech. You know how shy I am. I could never make a speech before a group of people."

Louis Howe smiled. "You've done many things you didn't think you could do. You'll learn to make speeches, too. I'll help you."

Eleanor was frightened during her first speech. When she saw Louis Howe in the back row, she was even more frightened. She felt just as she had years before, when she saw her mother in the back of the schoolroom. "He frightens me the way Mama did," she thought. "He'll be disappointed in me, too."

Louis Howe was waiting for Eleanor when she finished speaking. Eleanor didn't know whether to laugh or cry. She could tell by his face that she hadn't done very well.

"I can tell you're going to scold me," she said, "the way my mother did when I was a little girl. I know I was terrible."

"You weren't very good," he answered.

"I was frightened," Eleanor said.

"Your voice was too high," he went on. "You

spoke too long. You laughed at the end of sentences when there wasn't anything whatever to laugh about."

"That was because I was nervous."

"You must learn not to be nervous. There's no reason to be nervous," Louis Howe declared. He was much shorter than Eleanor. He had to look up at her as they walked down the street. "There are three rules to remember when you make a speech. Have something you want to say. Say it. Then sit down."

"Didn't I do anything right?" Eleanor asked.

Louis Howe looked up at her. "You look very nice on the stage," he said. "You manage to look friendly and dignified at the same time. And your hands are wonderful. They seem to tell people how you really feel."

Eleanor listened carefully to everything Louis Howe told her. Bit by bit her speeches became better. After a while she had many invitations to speak. There were so many she had to refuse most of them. Finally she became one of the best women speakers in the country.

Bit by bit Franklin was improving, too. At first he wasn't able to move his legs at all. He spent months trying to move his toes again. He spent hours crawling on the floor. He exercised every day. He was able to swim again, too. In many ways he was stronger and healthier than he had ever been before.

Finally, with heavy braces and additional support, he was able to walk short distances. However, walking was always difficult and painful. He had to spend most of his time sitting in a wheel chair.

In 1929 Franklin Roosevelt became Governor of New York State. As he and Eleanor rode to the executive mansion in Albany, New York, Franklin took Eleanor's hand and said, "Since it is difficult for me to walk, there are many places where I won't be able to go. You will have to be my eyes and my ears."

Eleanor had many duties as the wife of the Governor. She had to meet and entertain many groups of people. She had to meet and entertain important people who came to Albany.

Eleanor had other interests too. In 1926 many of the farmers who lived near Hyde Park were out of work. Eleanor and two of her friends decided to build a furniture factory. Then they taught the farmers how to make hand-made furniture.

Neither Eleanor nor her friends received any pay or profits from the factory. All the profits were given to the men who made the furniture.

The next year Eleanor and two other friends bought a private girls' school in New York City. Eleanor became vice-principal. She had always wanted to be a teacher. Now she taught American history, English, and American literature.

After they moved to Albany, Eleanor went to New York City three days a week so she could continue to teach.

Even with all these interests and duties, Eleanor still found time to be Franklin's "eyes and ears." She traveled all over the state. She talked with many people. She visited state schools and parks. She visited hospitals and prisons. She looked at the rooms where people slept. She looked into their kettles and tasted their food. Then she reported what she had seen and heard to her husband.

Eleanor and Franklin worked together as a team. Together they tried to do what they could for people who needed help and encouragement.

The White House

On March 4, 1933, Franklin D. Roosevelt became President of the United States. The streets of Washington, D.C., were lined with people who wanted to see the new President. They cheered as he and his wife rode to the White House, which was to be their new home.

At this time the country was in the depths of a great depression. Many people were out of work. As Eleanor and Franklin waved to the people, they noticed that many were poorly dressed. Many looked thin and hungry. Many looked bewildered and frightened.

Once more Franklin took Eleanor's hand.

"Now, more than ever," he said, "you will have to be my eyes and ears."

Franklin Roosevelt wanted to be President of all the people—the farmers, the factory workers, the miners, the fishermen, the storekeepers, the artists, the writers, the musicians, the poor and the rich.

After Franklin D. Roosevelt became President, things began to change in the United States. People began to feel that the President and his wife cared about them and their problems. They were encouraged by the things the President did to create more jobs. They knew the First Lady was interested, too. She was never too busy to try to help people.

Now Eleanor traveled all over the United States, by car, by bus, by train, by plane—often alone. Now she became the eyes and ears of the President of the United States.

Finally there were more jobs, more food, more

new houses. This, in turn, meant more jobs for more people—more food—more new houses. The United States was on its way again.

Eleanor did many things no other First Lady had done. She had regular press conferences for women reporters. She invited people to the White House who had never been invited before —Negroes, labor leaders, young people with special problems, unfortunate people who needed help. She wanted the President to hear what these people had to say.

Eleanor lectured and spoke on the radio. She wrote books and articles and a column called "My Day," which was printed in over 90 newspapers. She gave away most of the money she earned.

Some people thought it was undignified for the wife of the President to do these things. This was Eleanor's reply. "The money I earn can save thousands of lives. I don't value my dignity that highly. The people I can help with the money I earn are much more important."

On June 7, 1938, The King and Queen of England visited the United States. The President and his wife met them in Washington.

There were a number of state dinners. Then the King and Queen were invited to visit the Roosevelts at Hyde Park.

The King and Queen arrived one evening in time for dinner. While they were eating the first course, there was a loud rumble, then a terrible crash. A serving table piled high with dishes fell to the floor.

The President's mother had borrowed some dishes from another Mrs. Roosevelt who lived next door. When the table fell, the other Mrs. Roosevelt, who had loaned the dishes, said in a loud whisper, "Oh, I hope my dishes weren't broken." Eleanor's mother-in-law was very embarrassed, but Eleanor was amused.

After dinner the guests went into the library. A few minutes later a butler hurried down the hall, carrying a large tray of glasses and bowls of ice. He was a butler from the White House who had never been at Hyde Park before. He misjudged the steps between the hall and the library, stumbled, and fell.

Crash! The tray fell with him. Thousands of pieces of glass and ice covered the floor. At the foot of the steps was a small pool of water. Slipping on the glass, ice, and water, the butler slid into the library on his back. Finally he stopped in front of the Queen.

Getting to his feet, he walked out of the room as if nothing had happened. The Queen pretended not to notice, but Eleanor could scarcely keep from laughing.

The next day people came from far and near to Hyde Park to meet the King and Queen and to have a picnic. Eleanor served hot dogs and smoked turkey, which the King and Queen had not tasted before. She served several kinds of ham cured in different ways, from different parts of the United States. She also had salads, baked beans, and strawberry shortcake.

Many people thought it was undignified to serve hot dogs to the King and Queen of England. Eleanor thought differently. She was sure they were tired of formal state dinners, and she wanted them to taste typical American food.

Later that afternoon the President and the King had a swim together. Then Eleanor and her secretary brought out a large cart filled with glasses, cups, saucers, plates, a teapot, cream, sugar, and a large plate of cookies.

Finally they were all ready to have tea. Then Franklin, who was talking to the Queen, leaned against the cart. Crash! There was the familiar sound of breaking dishes. The contents of the cart covered the ground.

This time everyone had to laugh. After three enjoyable days together they were able to laugh together, like old friends.

On December 7, 1941, the Japanese attacked Pearl Harbor. The next day the United States entered the Second World War.

Now Eleanor traveled thousands of miles overseas to visit men in the armed forces. She went to camps and hospitals. She talked to the men and often took the names and addresses of their families. When she got back she called or wrote to their wives or parents.

Many people didn't understand why Eleanor traveled so much. They thought she should stay close to the White House as other First Ladies had done. She paid no attention to the things these people said about her. She knew that, once again, she was being her husband's "eyes and ears." She knew that, once again, she and her husband were working together as a team.

The United Nations

PRESIDENT ROOSEVELT died on April 12, 1945, in Warm Springs, Georgia.

When Vice President Truman came to the White House to see Eleanor, he could scarcely speak. "What can I do?" he asked.

"Tell us what we can do for you," she replied. "Is there any way we can help you?"

The months that followed her husband's death were very difficult for Eleanor. However, her first thought was always of what she could do to help others.

The Roosevelt family gave the big house at Hyde Park to the United States government. It became a national museum. Eleanor moved to a small cottage nearby. She planned to live a quiet life. Her children were grown and married. For the first time she was alone.

One day President Truman called Eleanor. He asked her to be a United States representative to the United Nations. When she agreed, he asked her to represent the United States at the Human Rights meeting in England.

Eleanor and her husband had been disappointed when the United States didn't join the League of Nations. Now she had a chance to work with this new organization for world peace and the betterment of all people.

She worked hard in England. She read many papers and articles. She talked with a great many people. She never missed a meeting, even though she was ill part of the time.

During this meeting an English woman said, "Eleanor Roosevelt cares first and always for people . . . her interest is human beings . . . her hobby is human beings . . . her every thought is for human beings . . . every single thing she devotes herself to has to do with human beings of one sort or another . . . the basis of all her strength is her interest in people."

Eleanor Roosevelt became chairperson of the Human Rights Commission. It became one of the important committees of the United Nations. When the Universal Declaration of Human Rights was passed, a headline in the *New York Times* called this ELEANOR ROOSEVELT'S VICTORY.

Once more Eleanor began to travel. She visited countries all over the world. She wanted to see for herself how people lived. She wanted to eat the food they ate. She wanted to know what they thought. Now she was using her eyes and ears to help the United Nations.

When Eleanor was at home in her little cot-

tage, the great and the humble of the world came to see her. Farmers, factory workers, students, kings and queens, princes and princesses, emperors, premiers, presidents, and sheiks, all came to talk with her. She always listened to them more than she talked.

Eleanor Roosevelt became the world's most admired and talked-about woman. To the world, she was Eleanor. The name Roosevelt was known throughout the world. After a while the name Eleanor became almost as well known.

When Eleanor Roosevelt died delegates from the Soviet bloc, Africa, Asia, Latin America, and Europe joined in expressing admiration for the "First Lady of the World."

In Washington, D.C., and in many states throughout the country, the United States flag on state and federal buildings was flown at half mast. It was the first time such an honor had been paid to the wife of a former president.

The United Nations president, Muhammed Khan, asked the delegates to stand in silent tribute. Outside the building, the United Nations blue and white flag was flown at half mast. This tribute had been paid to only one other person—Secretary General Dag Hammarskjold, who had died the year before.

Adlai Stevenson, the United States Ambassador to the United Nations, spoke first.

He said, "The United States, the United Nations—the world—has lost one of its great citizens. The United Nations is a memorial to Eleanor Roosevelt. To it she gave the last fifteen years of her restless life. She breathed life into this organization."

So many people wanted to speak that some had to speak for groups of countries. Taieb Slim said, "We in Africa have lost a friend."

Mrs. Agda Rossel of Sweden said, "Mrs. Roosevelt enriched the lives of all who knew her. The women of the world have a special gratitude to her for all she taught us, for all the encouragement she gave to women all over the world in their endeavors."

Katsue Okazaki of Japan said, "We grieve because the entire Japanese people had come to know and love her."

Carlet Auguste of Haiti said, "In every capital of Latin America, this tragic loss is felt."

Valerian Zorin of Russia said, "The death of Mrs. Roosevelt removed something from the lives of each one of us. She was allied deeply to the cause of peace."

Later Mr. Stevenson said, "Where she walked, beauty was always there." He also said, "She did not despair of the darkness. She lit a candle. Her glow has warmed the world."

As long as people want to help one another—as long as people work for peace—her glow will continue to warm the world.